GOSCINNY AND UDERZO
PRESENT
*An Asterix Adventure*

# ASTERIX
# THE
# GAUL

*Written by* RENÉ GOSCINNY *and Illustrated by* ALBERT UDERZO

*Translated by* Anthea Bell *and* Derek Hockridge

ORION

© 1961 GOSCINNY/UDERZO
Revised edition and English translation © 2004 HACHETTE

Original title: *Astérix Le Gaulois*

████████████████████████

Exclusive Licensee: Orion Publishing Group
Translators: Anthea Bell and Derek Hockridge
Typography: Bryony Newhouse

████████████████████████

This revised edition first published in 2004 by
Orion Books Ltd
Orion House, 5 Upper St Martin's Lane
London WC2H 9EA

Printed in France by Partenaires

www.asterix.tm.fr

A CIP catalogue record for this book is available from the British Library

ISBN 0 752866044 (cased)
ISBN 0 752866052 (paperback)

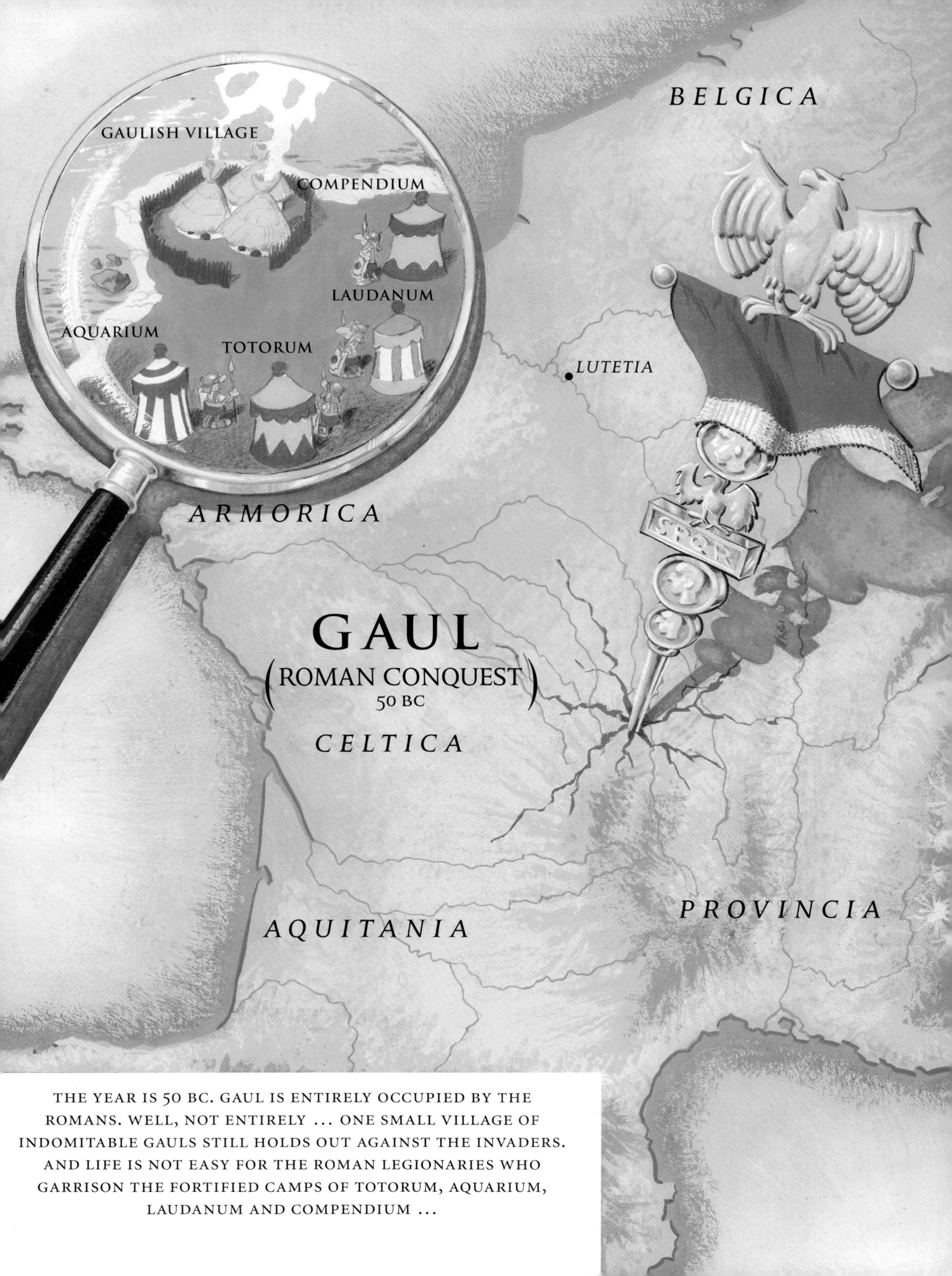
BELGICA
GAULISH VILLAGE
COMPENDIUM
LAUDANUM
AQUARIUM
TOTORUM
LUTETIA
SPQR
ARMORICA
GAUL
(ROMAN CONQUEST
50 BC)
CELTICA
PROVINCIA
AQUITANIA

THE YEAR IS 50 BC. GAUL IS ENTIRELY OCCUPIED BY THE ROMANS. WELL, NOT ENTIRELY ... ONE SMALL VILLAGE OF INDOMITABLE GAULS STILL HOLDS OUT AGAINST THE INVADERS. AND LIFE IS NOT EASY FOR THE ROMAN LEGIONARIES WHO GARRISON THE FORTIFIED CAMPS OF TOTORUM, AQUARIUM, LAUDANUM AND COMPENDIUM ...

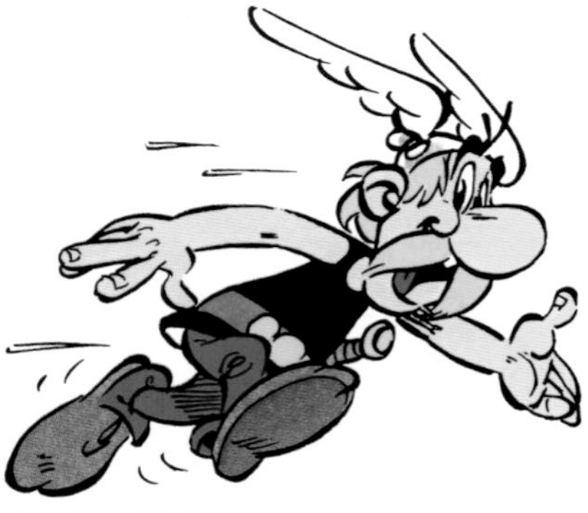

ASTERIX, THE HERO OF THESE ADVENTURES. A SHREWD, CUNNING LITTLE WARRIOR, ALL PERILOUS MISSIONS ARE IMMEDIATELY ENTRUSTED TO HIM. ASTERIX GETS HIS SUPERHUMAN STRENGTH FROM THE MAGIC POTION BREWED BY THE DRUID GETAFIX . . .

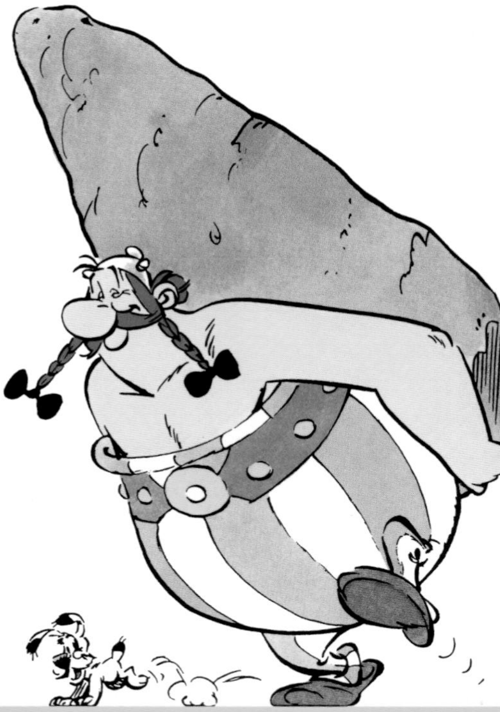

OBELIX, ASTERIX'S INSEPARABLE FRIEND. A MENHIR DELIVERY MAN BY TRADE, ADDICTED TO WILD BOAR. OBELIX IS ALWAYS READY TO DROP EVERYTHING AND GO OFF ON A NEW ADVENTURE WITH ASTERIX – SO LONG AS THERE'S WILD BOAR TO EAT, AND PLENTY OF FIGHTING. HIS CONSTANT COMPANION IS DOGMATIX, THE ONLY KNOWN CANINE ECOLOGIST, WHO HOWLS WITH DESPAIR WHEN A TREE IS CUT DOWN.

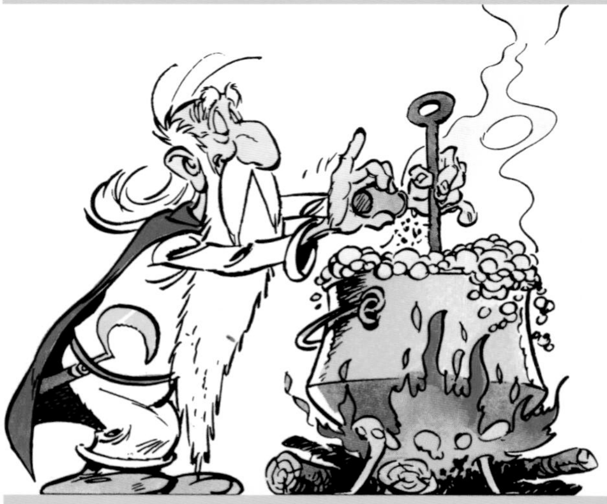

GETAFIX, THE VENERABLE VILLAGE DRUID, GATHERS MISTLETOE AND BREWS MAGIC POTIONS. HIS SPECIALITY IS THE POTION WHICH GIVES THE DRINKER SUPERHUMAN STRENGTH. BUT GETAFIX ALSO HAS OTHER RECIPES UP HIS SLEEVE . . .

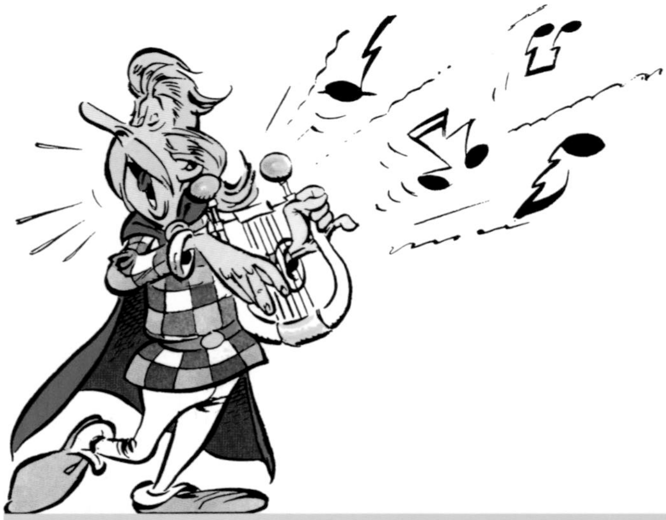

CACOFONIX, THE BARD. OPINION IS DIVIDED AS TO HIS MUSICAL GIFTS. CACOFONIX THINKS HE'S A GENIUS. EVERYONE ELSE THINKS HE'S UNSPEAKABLE. BUT SO LONG AS HE DOESN'T SPEAK, LET ALONE SING, EVERYBODY LIKES HIM . . .

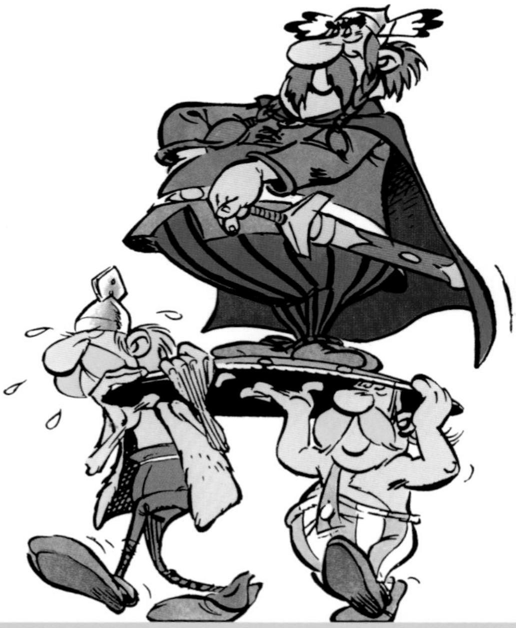

FINALLY, VITALSTATISTIX, THE CHIEF OF THE TRIBE. MAJESTIC, BRAVE AND HOT-TEMPERED, THE OLD WARRIOR IS RESPECTED BY HIS MEN AND FEARED BY HIS ENEMIES. VITALSTATISTIX HIMSELF HAS ONLY ONE FEAR, HE IS AFRAID THE SKY MAY FALL ON HIS HEAD TOMORROW. BUT AS HE ALWAYS SAYS, TOMORROW NEVER COMES.

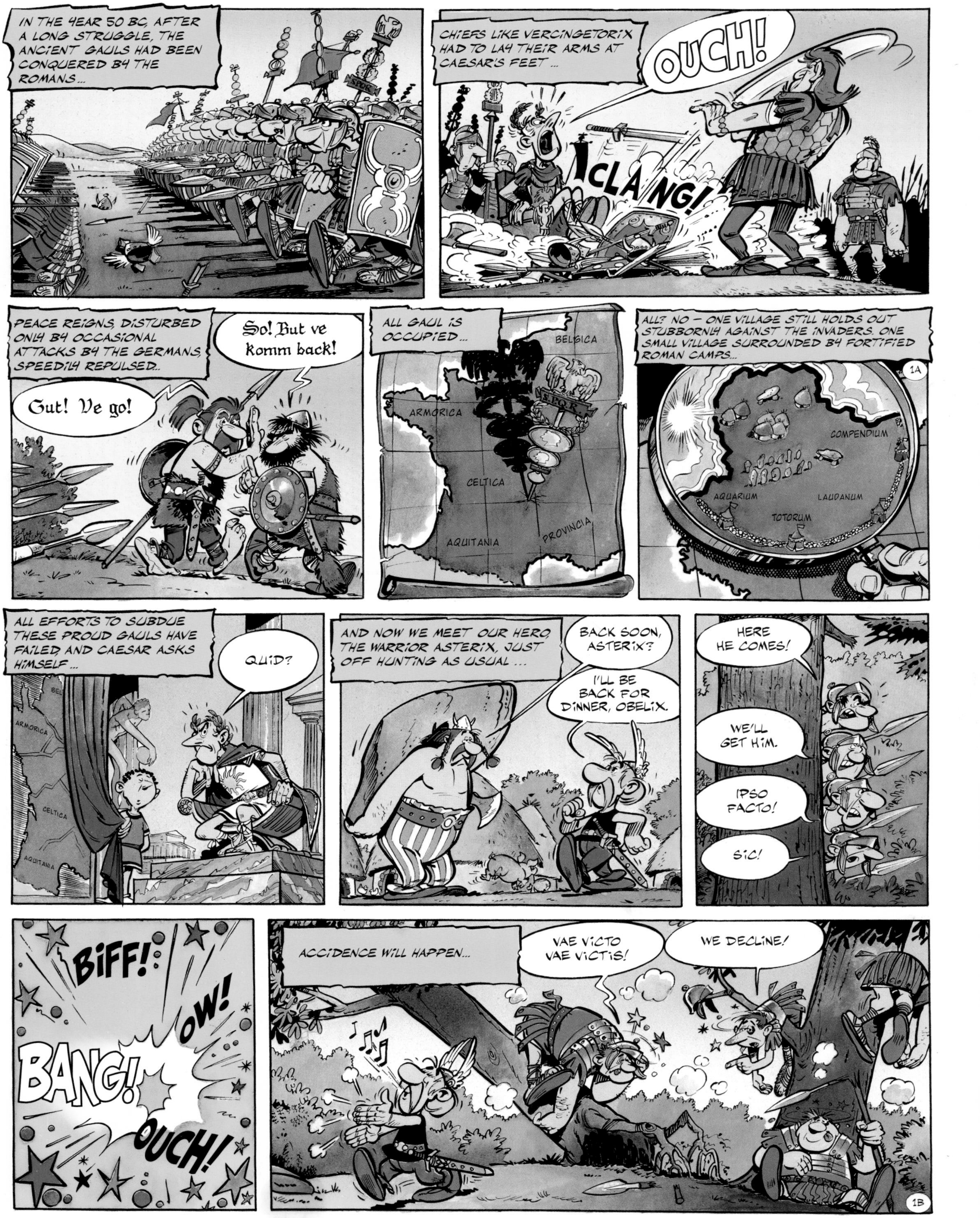
IN THE YEAR 50 BC, AFTER A LONG STRUGGLE, THE ANCIENT GAULS HAD BEEN CONQUERED BY THE ROMANS...
CHIEFS LIKE VERCINGETORIX HAD TO LAY THEIR ARMS AT CAESAR'S FEET ...
OUCH!
CLANG!
PEACE REIGNS, DISTURBED ONLY BY OCCASIONAL ATTACKS BY THE GERMANS, SPEEDILY REPULSED...
So! But ve komm back!
Gut! Ve go!
ALL GAUL IS OCCUPIED ...
BELGICA
ARMORICA
CELTICA
AQUITANIA
PROVINCIA
ALL? NO — ONE VILLAGE STILL HOLDS OUT STUBBORNLY AGAINST THE INVADERS. ONE SMALL VILLAGE SURROUNDED BY FORTIFIED ROMAN CAMPS...
1A
COMPENDIUM
AQUARIUM
LAUDANUM
TOTORUM
ALL EFFORTS TO SUBDUE THESE PROUD GAULS HAVE FAILED, AND CAESAR ASKS HIMSELF ...
QUID?
AND NOW WE MEET OUR HERO, THE WARRIOR ASTERIX, JUST OFF HUNTING AS USUAL ...
BACK SOON, ASTERIX?
I'LL BE BACK FOR DINNER, OBELIX.
HERE HE COMES!
WE'LL GET HIM.
IPSO FACTO!
SIC!
BIFF!
OW!
BANG!
OUCH!
ACCIDENCE WILL HAPPEN...
VAE VICTO VAE VICTIS!
WE DECLINE!
1B

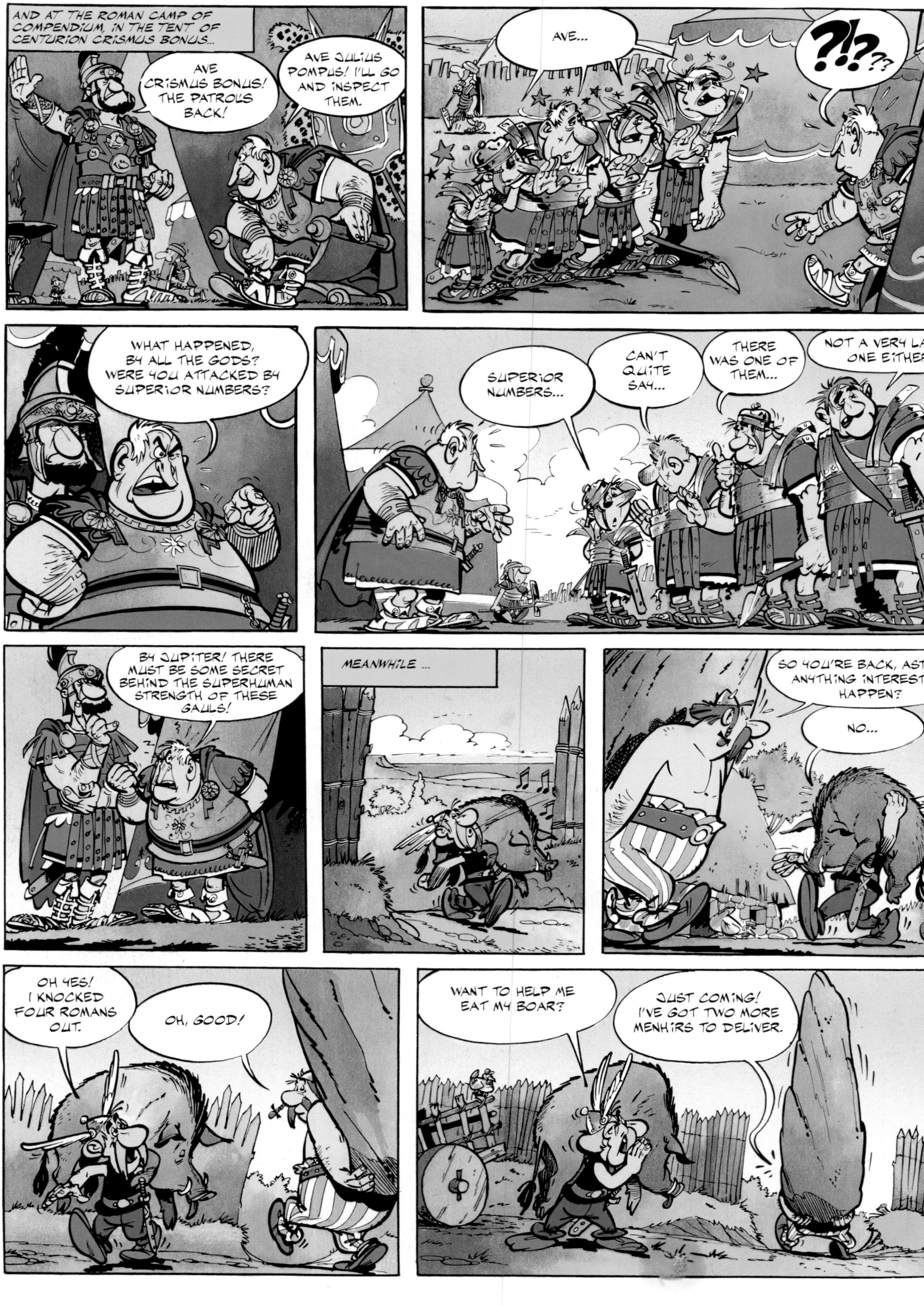

AND AT THE ROMAN CAMP OF COMPENDIUM, IN THE TENT OF CENTURION CRISMUS BONUS...
AVE CRISMUS BONUS! THE PATROL'S BACK!
AVE JULIUS POMPUS! I'LL GO AND INSPECT THEM.
AVE...
?!?????
WHAT HAPPENED, BY ALL THE GODS? WERE YOU ATTACKED BY SUPERIOR NUMBERS?
SUPERIOR NUMBERS...
CAN'T QUITE SAY...
THERE WAS ONE OF THEM...
NOT A VERY LARGE ONE EITHER!
2A
BY JUPITER! THERE MUST BE SOME SECRET BEHIND THE SUPERHUMAN STRENGTH OF THESE GAULS!
MEANWHILE ...
SO YOU'RE BACK, ASTERIX. ANYTHING INTERESTING HAPPEN?
NO...
OH YES! I KNOCKED FOUR ROMANS OUT.
OH, GOOD!
WANT TO HELP ME EAT MY BOAR?
JUST COMING! I'VE GOT TWO MORE MENHIRS TO DELIVER.
2B

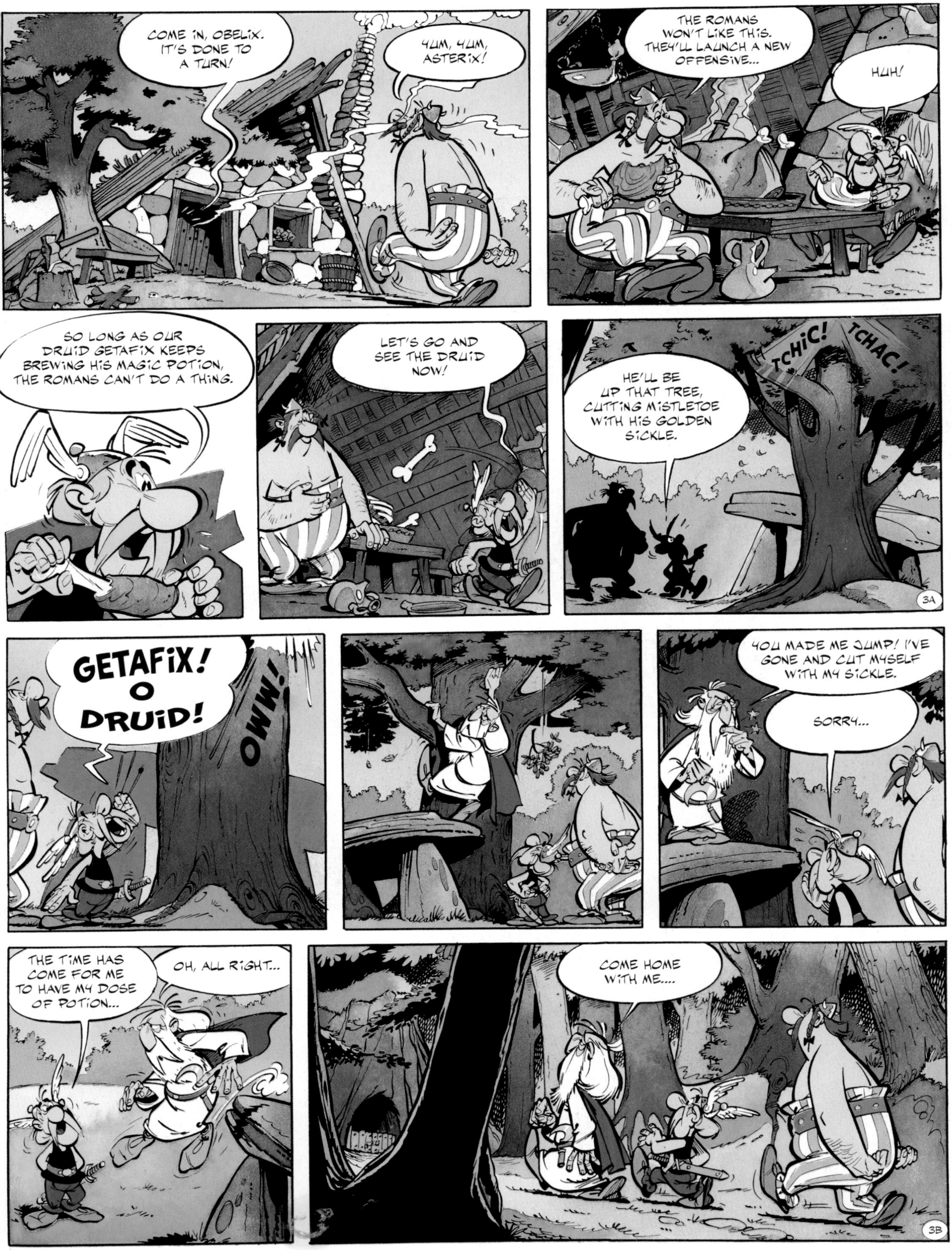

COME IN, OBELIX. IT'S DONE TO A TURN!
YUM, YUM, ASTERIX!
THE ROMANS WON'T LIKE THIS. THEY'LL LAUNCH A NEW OFFENSIVE...
HUH!
SO LONG AS OUR DRUID GETAFIX KEEPS BREWING HIS MAGIC POTION, THE ROMANS CAN'T DO A THING.
LET'S GO AND SEE THE DRUID NOW!
TCHIC! TCHAC!
HE'LL BE UP THAT TREE, CUTTING MISTLETOE WITH HIS GOLDEN SICKLE.
3A
GETAFIX! O DRUID!
OWW!
YOU MADE ME JUMP! I'VE GONE AND CUT MYSELF WITH MY SICKLE.
SORRY...
THE TIME HAS COME FOR ME TO HAVE MY DOSE OF POTION...
OH, ALL RIGHT...
COME HOME WITH ME....
3B

HERE IS THE POTION THAT MAKES THE DRINKER INVINCIBLE! IT INCREASES HIS STRENGTH TENFOLD – FOR A LIMITED PERIOD OF TIME.

WHAT'S THE RECIPE, O DRUID?

THE ORIGIN OF THIS RECIPE IS LOST IN THE MISTS OF TIME. IT IS HANDED DOWN FROM DRUID TO DRUID BY WORD OF MOUTH...

ALL I CAN REVEAL IS THAT THERE'S MISTLETOE AND LOBSTER IN IT...

THE LOBSTER IS OPTIONAL, BUT IT IMPROVES THE FLAVOUR!

SPLOSH!

4A

CAN I HAVE SOME?

NO, OBELIX, YOU CAN NOT AND WELL YOU KNOW IT!

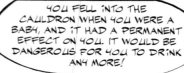

YOU FELL INTO THE CAULDRON WHEN YOU WERE A BABY, AND IT HAD A PERMANENT EFFECT ON YOU. IT WOULD BE DANGEROUS FOR YOU TO DRINK ANY MORE!

GLUG! GLUG! GLUG!

THANKS, O DRUID!

IT'S NOT FAIR, BY BELENOS!

OW! OW! OW!

I'VE TOLD YOU BEFORE NOT TO SHAKE HANDS WITH ME WHEN YOU'VE JUST HAD YOUR POTION.

HE'S RIGHT, I DON'T KNOW MY OWN STRENGTH!

4B

WE'VE BEEN LAYING SIEGE TO THESE GAULS FOR YEARS! THEY'VE GOT A NERVE! THIS MORNING'S PROVOCATION IS GOING TOO FAR. ONE AGAINST FOUR IS NO JOKE! THEY'RE MAKING US LOOK RIDICULOUS.
THERE'S SOME MYSTERY BEHIND THE STRENGTH OF THESE GAULS. WE MUST LEARN THEIR SECRET.
YOU'RE RIGHT, MARCUS GINANTONICUS! WE MUST LEARN THEIR SECRET, AND FAST! CAESAR HAS INDICATED HIS DISPLEASURE ALL THE WAY FROM ROME. WE NEED A SPY IN THE GAULS' VILLAGE. I WANT A VOLUNTEER!
?!
5A
AS THERE ARE SO MANY VOLUNTEERS, WE'LL HAVE TO PLAY MUSICAL CHAIRS TO PICK THE SPY!
THIS ANCIENT ROMAN GAME IS PLAYED WITH ONE CHAIR FEWER THAN THERE ARE LEGIONARIES...
...WHEN THE MUSIC STOPS...
...ALL THE PLAYERS SIT DOWN. THE LEGIONARY WITHOUT A CHAIR HAS LOST.
CALIGULA MINUS IS OUT!
5B

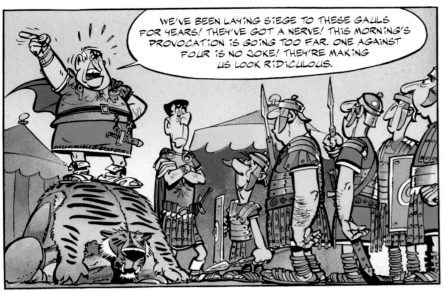

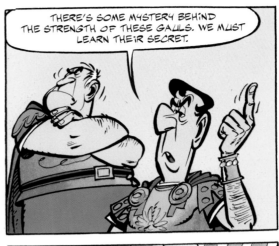

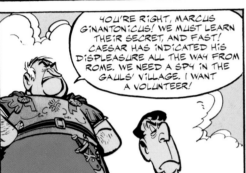

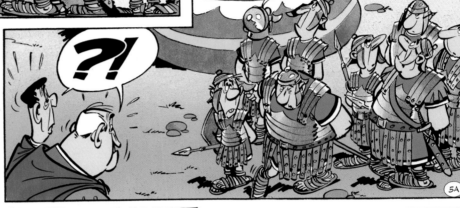

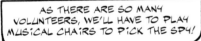

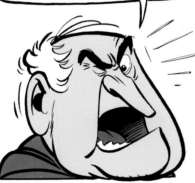

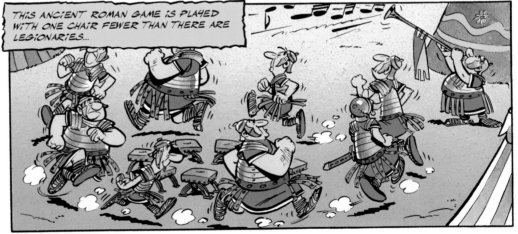

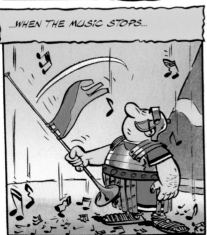

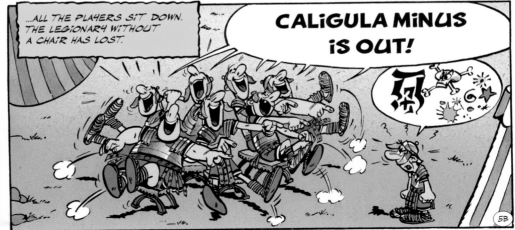

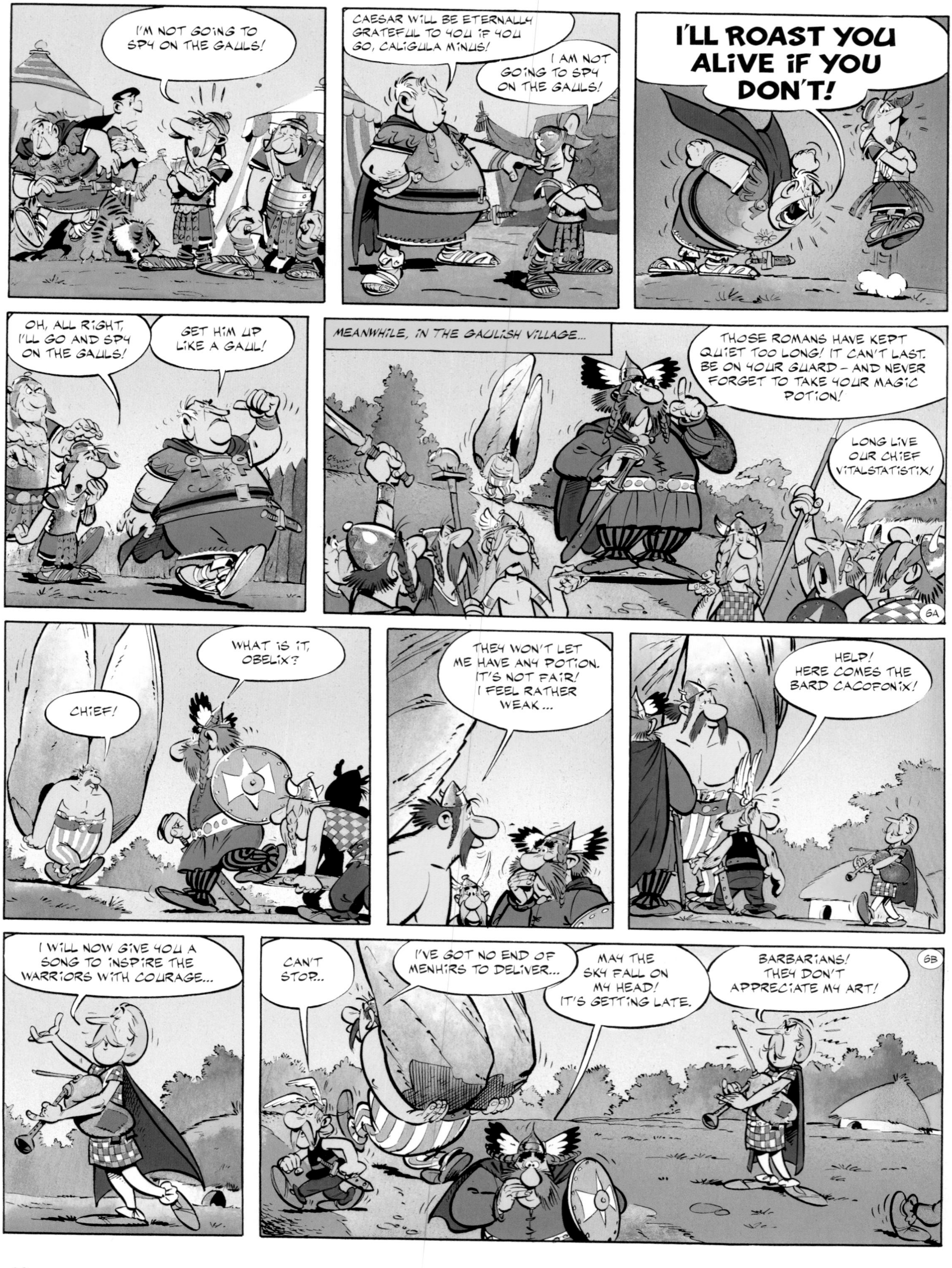
I'M NOT GOING TO SPY ON THE GAULS!
CAESAR WILL BE ETERNALLY GRATEFUL TO YOU IF YOU GO, CALIGULA MINUS!
I AM NOT GOING TO SPY ON THE GAULS!
I'LL ROAST YOU ALIVE IF YOU DON'T!
OH, ALL RIGHT, I'LL GO AND SPY ON THE GAULS!
GET HIM UP LIKE A GAUL!
MEANWHILE, IN THE GAULISH VILLAGE...
THOSE ROMANS HAVE KEPT QUIET TOO LONG! IT CAN'T LAST. BE ON YOUR GUARD – AND NEVER FORGET TO TAKE YOUR MAGIC POTION!
LONG LIVE OUR CHIEF VITALSTATISTIX!
6A
CHIEF!
WHAT IS IT, OBELIX?
THEY WON'T LET ME HAVE ANY POTION. IT'S NOT FAIR! I FEEL RATHER WEAK...
HELP! HERE COMES THE BARD CACOFONIX!
I WILL NOW GIVE YOU A SONG TO INSPIRE THE WARRIORS WITH COURAGE...
CAN'T STOP...
I'VE GOT NO END OF MENHIRS TO DELIVER...
MAY THE SKY FALL ON MY HEAD! IT'S GETTING LATE.
BARBARIANS! THEY DON'T APPRECIATE MY ART!
6B

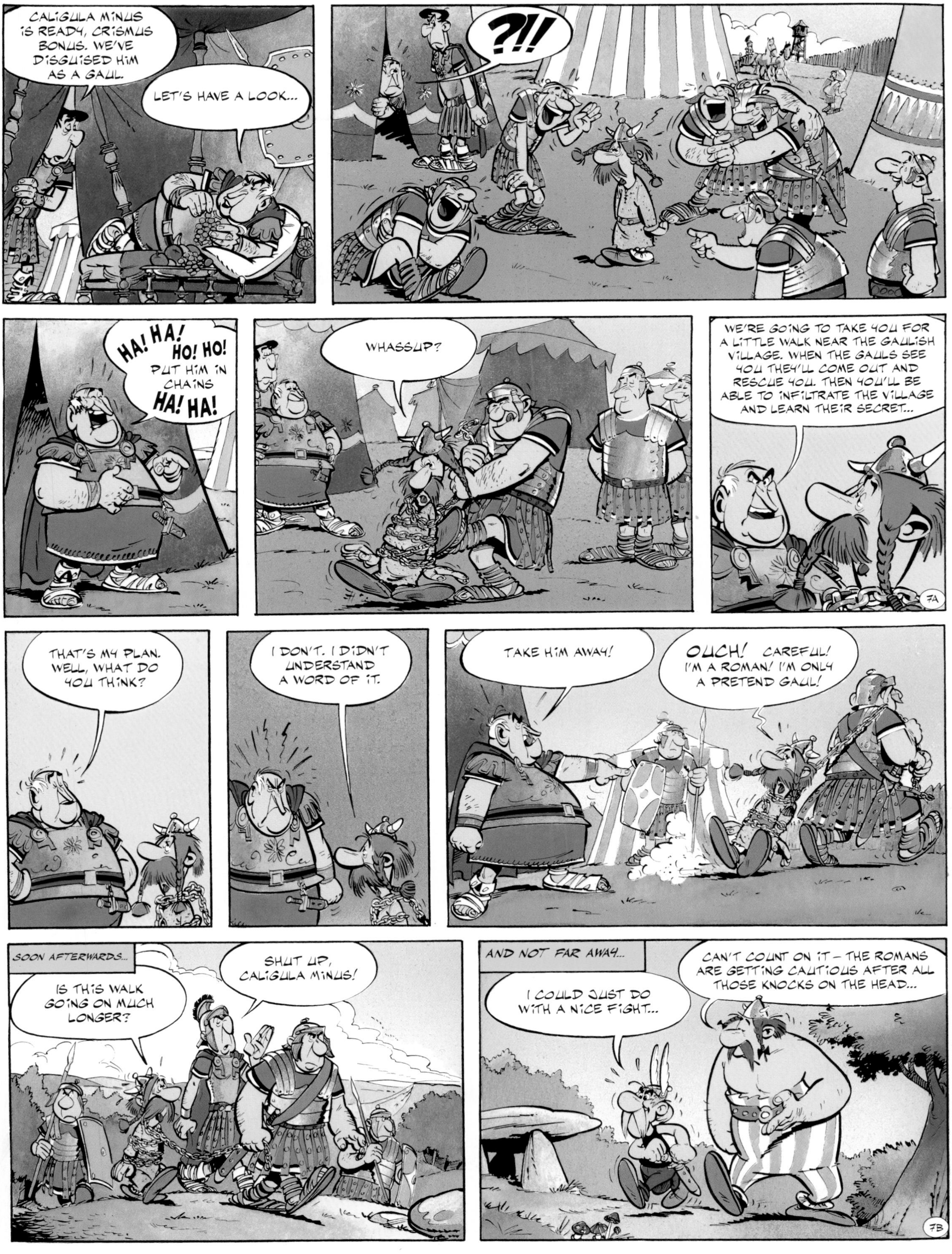
CALIGULA MINUS IS READY, CRISMUS BONUS. WE'VE DISGUISED HIM AS A GAUL.
LET'S HAVE A LOOK...
?!!
HA! HA! HO! HO! PUT HIM IN CHAINS HA! HA!
WHASSUP?
WE'RE GOING TO TAKE YOU FOR A LITTLE WALK NEAR THE GAULISH VILLAGE. WHEN THE GAULS SEE YOU THEY'LL COME OUT AND RESCUE YOU. THEN YOU'LL BE ABLE TO INFILTRATE THE VILLAGE AND LEARN THEIR SECRET...
7A
THAT'S MY PLAN. WELL, WHAT DO YOU THINK?
I DON'T. I DIDN'T UNDERSTAND A WORD OF IT.
TAKE HIM AWAY!
OUCH! CAREFUL! I'M A ROMAN! I'M ONLY A PRETEND GAUL!
SOON AFTERWARDS...
IS THIS WALK GOING ON MUCH LONGER?
SHUT UP, CALIGULA MINUS!
AND NOT FAR AWAY...
I COULD JUST DO WITH A NICE FIGHT...
CAN'T COUNT ON IT – THE ROMANS ARE GETTING CAUTIOUS AFTER ALL THOSE KNOCKS ON THE HEAD...
7B

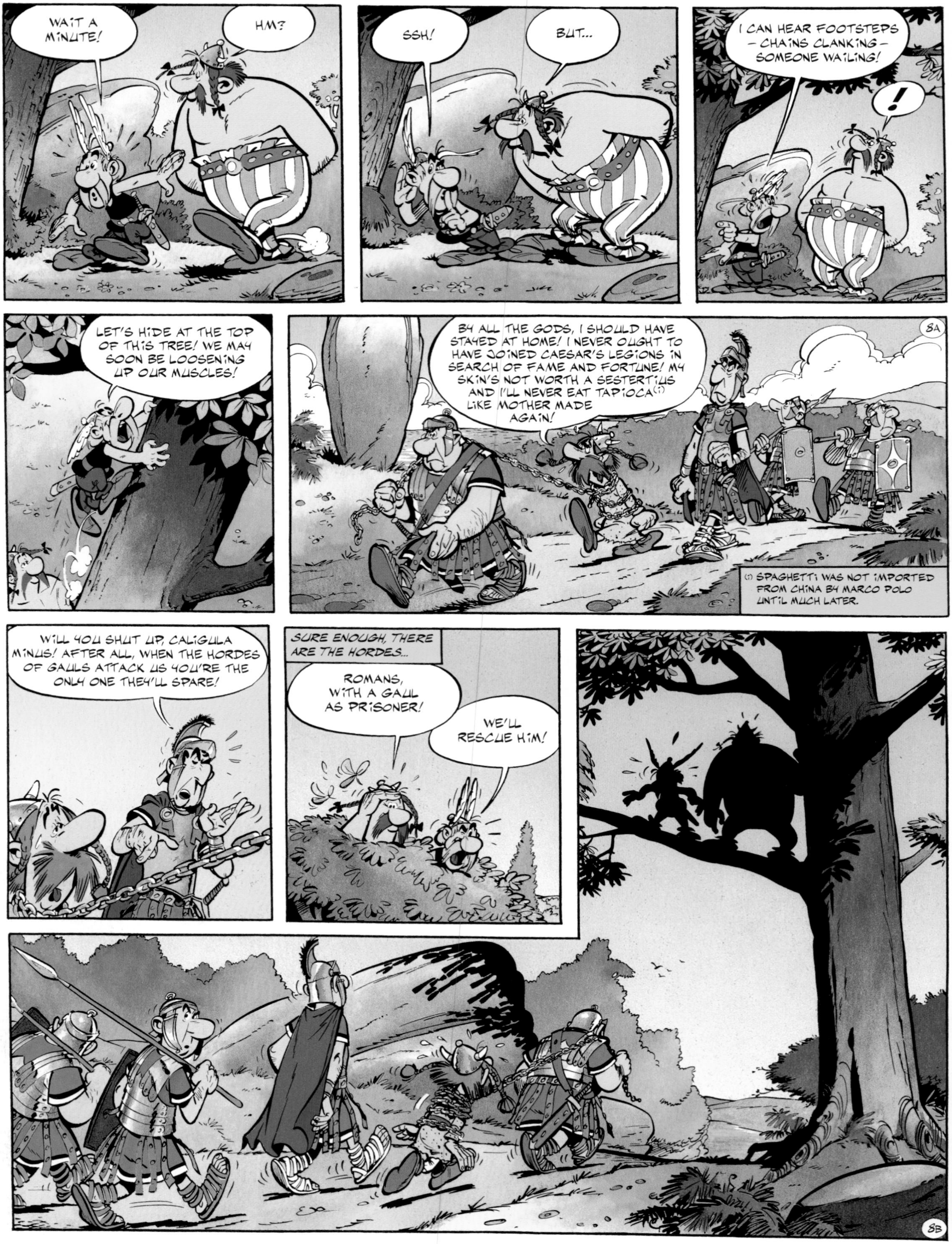
WAIT A MINUTE!
HM?
SSH!
BUT...
I CAN HEAR FOOTSTEPS – CHAINS CLANKING – SOMEONE WAILING!
!
LET'S HIDE AT THE TOP OF THIS TREE! WE MAY SOON BE LOOSENING UP OUR MUSCLES!
BY ALL THE GODS, I SHOULD HAVE STAYED AT HOME! I NEVER OUGHT TO HAVE JOINED CAESAR'S LEGIONS IN SEARCH OF FAME AND FORTUNE! MY SKIN'S NOT WORTH A SESTERTIUS AND I'LL NEVER EAT TAPIOCA(1) LIKE MOTHER MADE AGAIN!
8A
(1) SPAGHETTI WAS NOT IMPORTED FROM CHINA BY MARCO POLO UNTIL MUCH LATER.
WILL YOU SHUT UP, CALIGULA MINUS! AFTER ALL, WHEN THE HORDES OF GAULS ATTACK US YOU'RE THE ONLY ONE THEY'LL SPARE!
SURE ENOUGH, THERE ARE THE HORDES...
ROMANS, WITH A GAUL AS PRISONER!
WE'LL RESCUE HIM!
8B

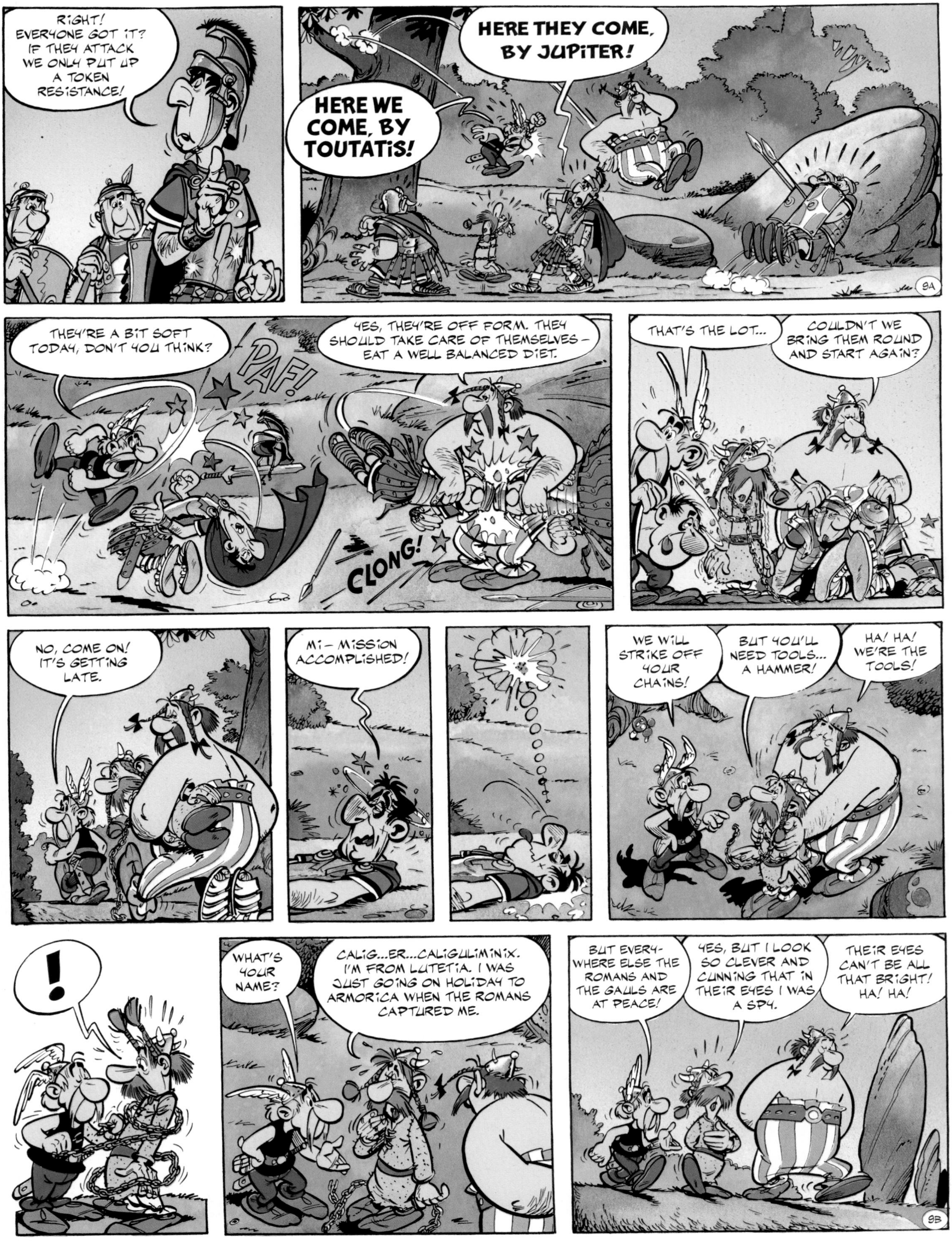
RIGHT! EVERYONE GOT IT? IF THEY ATTACK WE ONLY PUT UP A TOKEN RESISTANCE!
HERE THEY COME, BY JUPITER!
HERE WE COME, BY TOUTATIS!
9A
THEY'RE A BIT SOFT TODAY, DON'T YOU THINK?
PAF!
YES, THEY'RE OFF FORM. THEY SHOULD TAKE CARE OF THEMSELVES – EAT A WELL BALANCED DIET.
CLONG!
THAT'S THE LOT...
COULDN'T WE BRING THEM ROUND AND START AGAIN?
NO, COME ON! IT'S GETTING LATE.
MI– MISSION ACCOMPLISHED!
WE WILL STRIKE OFF YOUR CHAINS!
BUT YOU'LL NEED TOOLS... A HAMMER!
HA! HA! WE'RE THE TOOLS!
!
WHAT'S YOUR NAME?
CALIG...ER...CALIGULIMINIX. I'M FROM LUTETIA. I WAS JUST GOING ON HOLIDAY TO ARMORICA WHEN THE ROMANS CAPTURED ME.
BUT EVERY-WHERE ELSE THE ROMANS AND THE GAULS ARE AT PEACE!
YES, BUT I LOOK SO CLEVER AND CUNNING THAT IN THEIR EYES I WAS A SPY.
THEIR EYES CAN'T BE ALL THAT BRIGHT! HA! HA!
9B

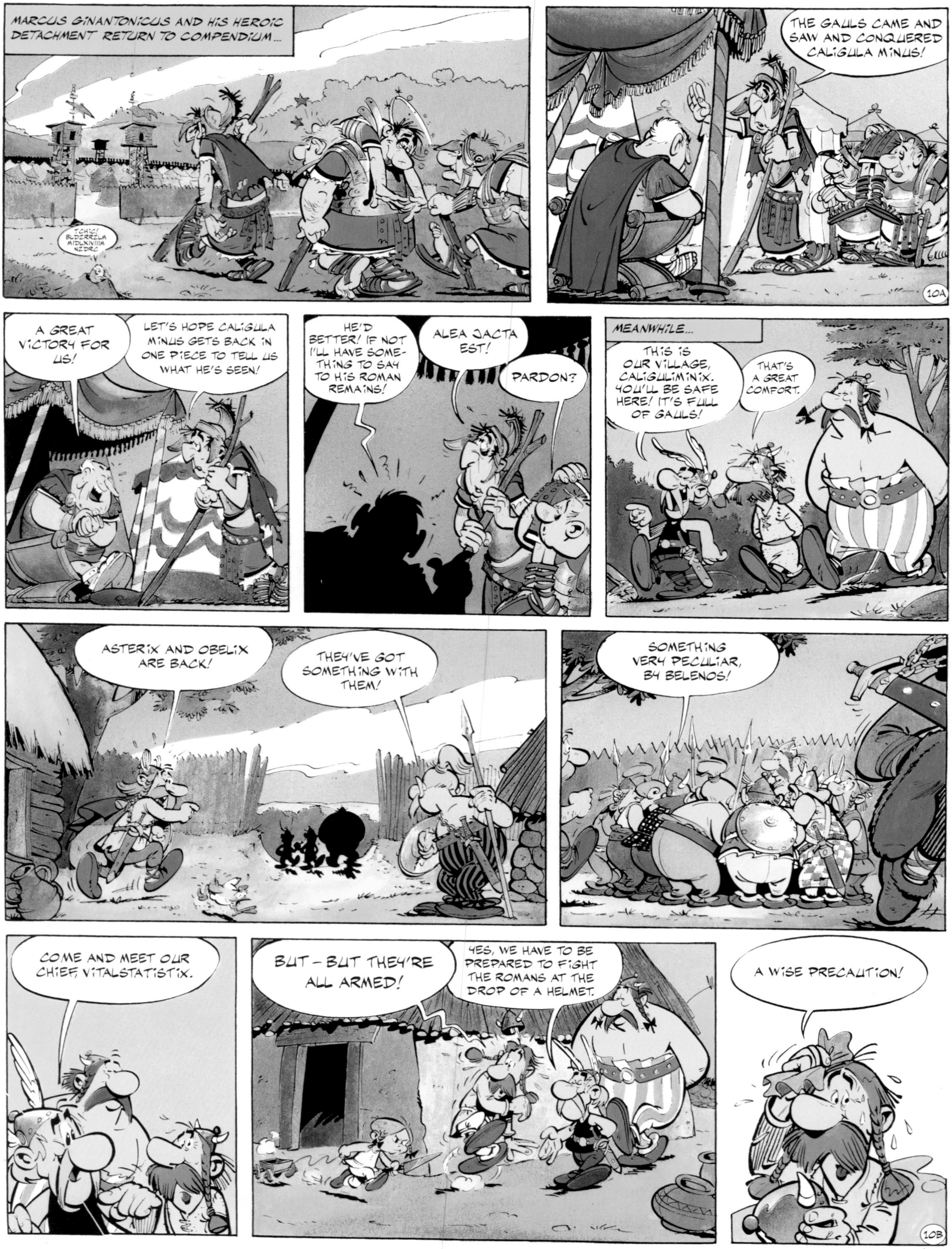
MARCUS GINANTONICUS AND HIS HEROIC DETACHMENT RETURN TO COMPENDIUM...
TCHIC! BLDZRRRZLM MIDLXIVIIIM NZDRC
THE GAULS CAME AND SAW AND CONQUERED CALIGULA MINUS!
10A
A GREAT VICTORY FOR US!
LET'S HOPE CALIGULA MINUS GETS BACK IN ONE PIECE TO TELL US WHAT HE'S SEEN!
HE'D BETTER! IF NOT I'LL HAVE SOMETHING TO SAY TO HIS ROMAN REMAINS!
ALEA JACTA EST!
PARDON?
MEANWHILE...
THIS IS OUR VILLAGE, CALIGULIMINIX. YOU'LL BE SAFE HERE! IT'S FULL OF GAULS!
THAT'S A GREAT COMFORT.
ASTERIX AND OBELIX ARE BACK!
THEY'VE GOT SOMETHING WITH THEM!
SOMETHING VERY PECULIAR, BY BELENOS!
COME AND MEET OUR CHIEF, VITALSTATISTIX.
BUT – BUT THEY'RE ALL ARMED!
YES, WE HAVE TO BE PREPARED TO FIGHT THE ROMANS AT THE DROP OF A HELMET.
A WISE PRECAUTION!
10B

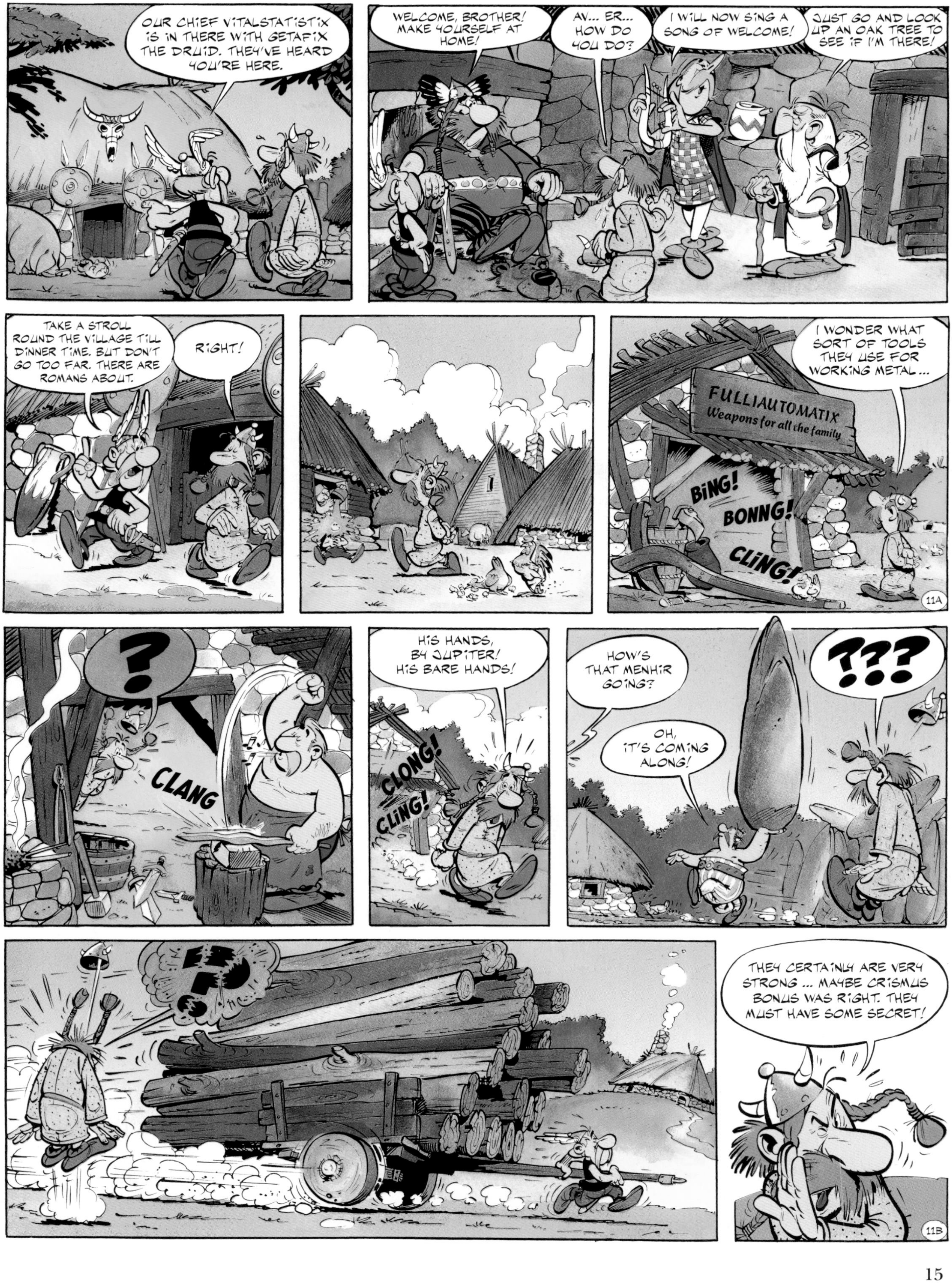
OUR CHIEF VITALSTATISTIX IS IN THERE WITH GETAFIX THE DRUID. THEY'VE HEARD YOU'RE HERE.
WELCOME, BROTHER! MAKE YOURSELF AT HOME!
AV... ER... HOW DO YOU DO?
I WILL NOW SING A SONG OF WELCOME!
JUST GO AND LOOK UP AN OAK TREE TO SEE IF I'M THERE!
TAKE A STROLL ROUND THE VILLAGE TILL DINNER TIME. BUT DON'T GO TOO FAR. THERE ARE ROMANS ABOUT.
RIGHT!
FULLIAUTOMATIX
Weapons for all the family
I WONDER WHAT SORT OF TOOLS THEY USE FOR WORKING METAL...
BING!
BONNG!
CLING!
?
CLANG
HIS HANDS, BY JUPITER! HIS BARE HANDS!
CLONG!
CLING!
HOW'S THAT MENHIR GOING?
OH, IT'S COMING ALONG!
???
THEY CERTAINLY ARE VERY STRONG ... MAYBE CRISMUS BONUS WAS RIGHT. THEY MUST HAVE SOME SECRET!

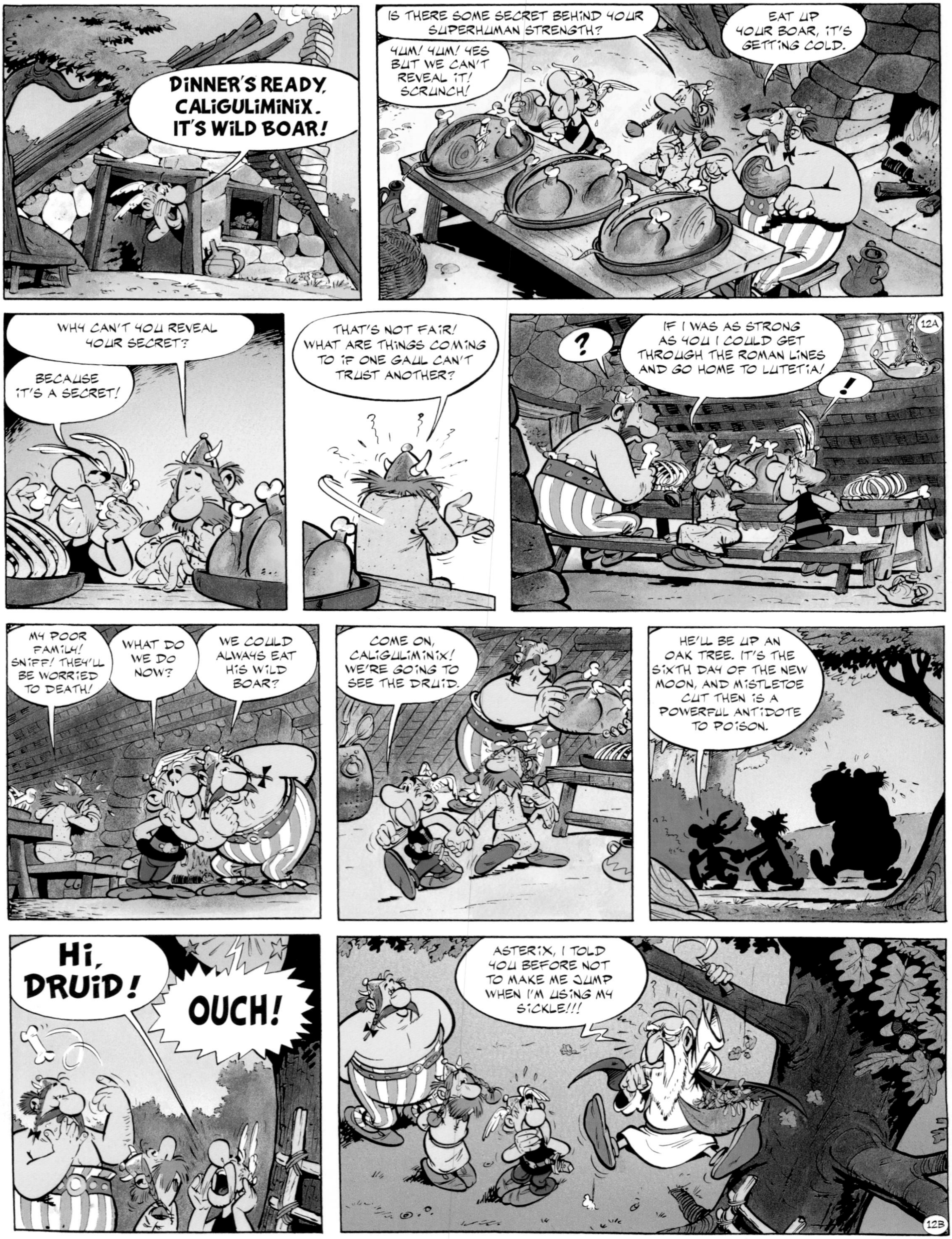
DINNER'S READY, CALIGULIMINIX. IT'S WILD BOAR!
IS THERE SOME SECRET BEHIND YOUR SUPERHUMAN STRENGTH?
YUM! YUM! YES BUT WE CAN'T REVEAL IT! SCRUNCH!
EAT UP YOUR BOAR, IT'S GETTING COLD.
WHY CAN'T YOU REVEAL YOUR SECRET?
BECAUSE IT'S A SECRET!
THAT'S NOT FAIR! WHAT ARE THINGS COMING TO IF ONE GAUL CAN'T TRUST ANOTHER?
12A
?
IF I WAS AS STRONG AS YOU I COULD GET THROUGH THE ROMAN LINES AND GO HOME TO LUTETIA!
!
MY POOR FAMILY! SNIFF! THEY'LL BE WORRIED TO DEATH!
WHAT DO WE DO NOW?
WE COULD ALWAYS EAT HIS WILD BOAR?
COME ON, CALIGULIMINIX! WE'RE GOING TO SEE THE DRUID.
HE'LL BE UP AN OAK TREE. IT'S THE SIXTH DAY OF THE NEW MOON, AND MISTLETOE CUT THEN IS A POWERFUL ANTIDOTE TO POISON.
HI, DRUID!
OUCH!
ASTERIX, I TOLD YOU BEFORE NOT TO MAKE ME JUMP WHEN I'M USING MY SICKLE!!!
12B

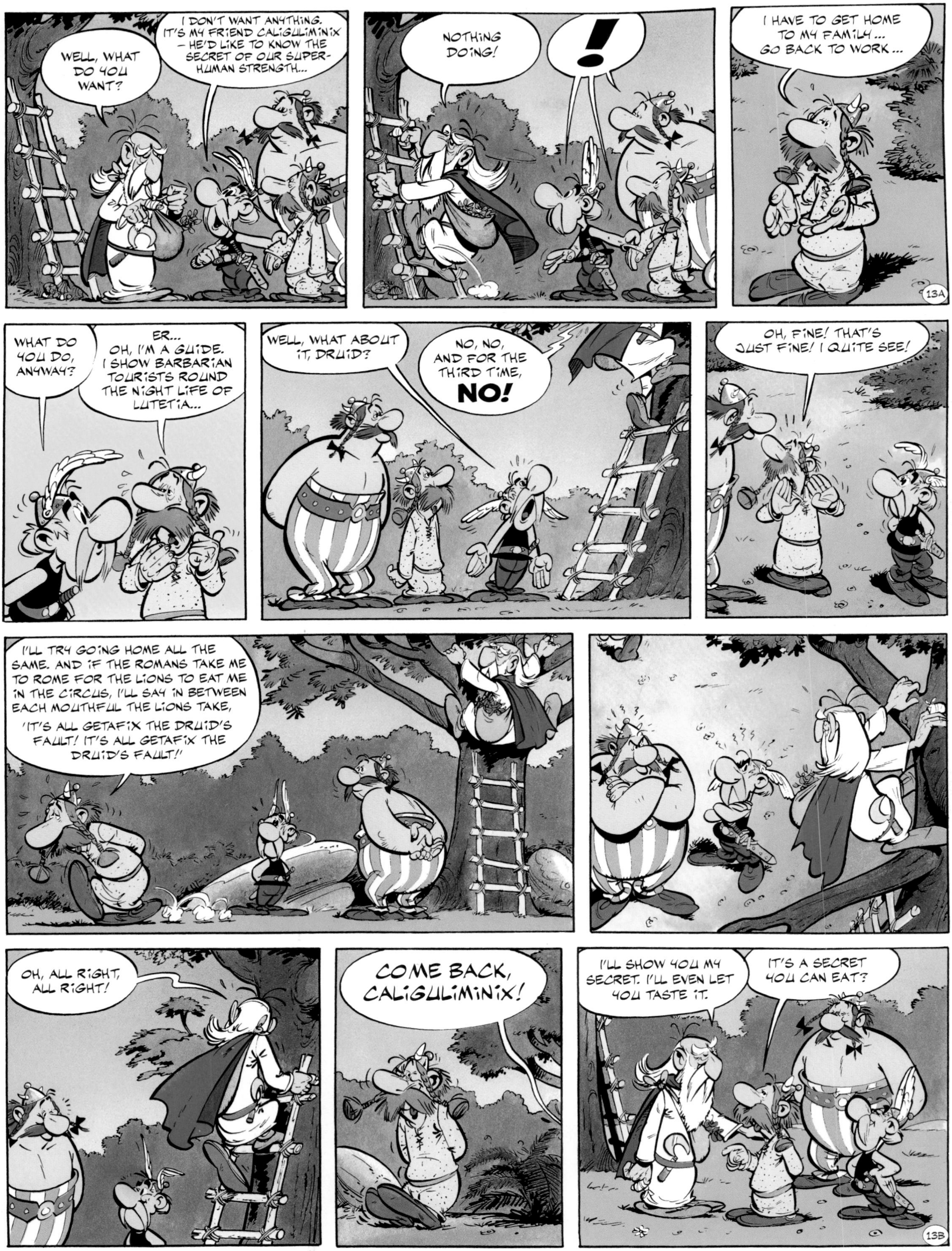
WELL, WHAT DO YOU WANT?
I DON'T WANT ANYTHING. IT'S MY FRIEND CALIGULIMINIX – HE'D LIKE TO KNOW THE SECRET OF OUR SUPER-HUMAN STRENGTH...
NOTHING DOING!
!
I HAVE TO GET HOME TO MY FAMILY... GO BACK TO WORK...
13A
WHAT DO YOU DO, ANYWAY?
ER... OH, I'M A GUIDE. I SHOW BARBARIAN TOURISTS ROUND THE NIGHT LIFE OF LUTETIA...
WELL, WHAT ABOUT IT, DRUID?
NO, NO, AND FOR THE THIRD TIME, NO!
OH, FINE! THAT'S JUST FINE! I QUITE SEE!
I'LL TRY GOING HOME ALL THE SAME. AND IF THE ROMANS TAKE ME TO ROME FOR THE LIONS TO EAT ME IN THE CIRCUS, I'LL SAY IN BETWEEN EACH MOUTHFUL THE LIONS TAKE, 'IT'S ALL GETAFIX THE DRUID'S FAULT! IT'S ALL GETAFIX THE DRUID'S FAULT!'
OH, ALL RIGHT, ALL RIGHT!
COME BACK, CALIGULIMINIX!
I'LL SHOW YOU MY SECRET. I'LL EVEN LET YOU TASTE IT.
IT'S A SECRET YOU CAN EAT?
13B

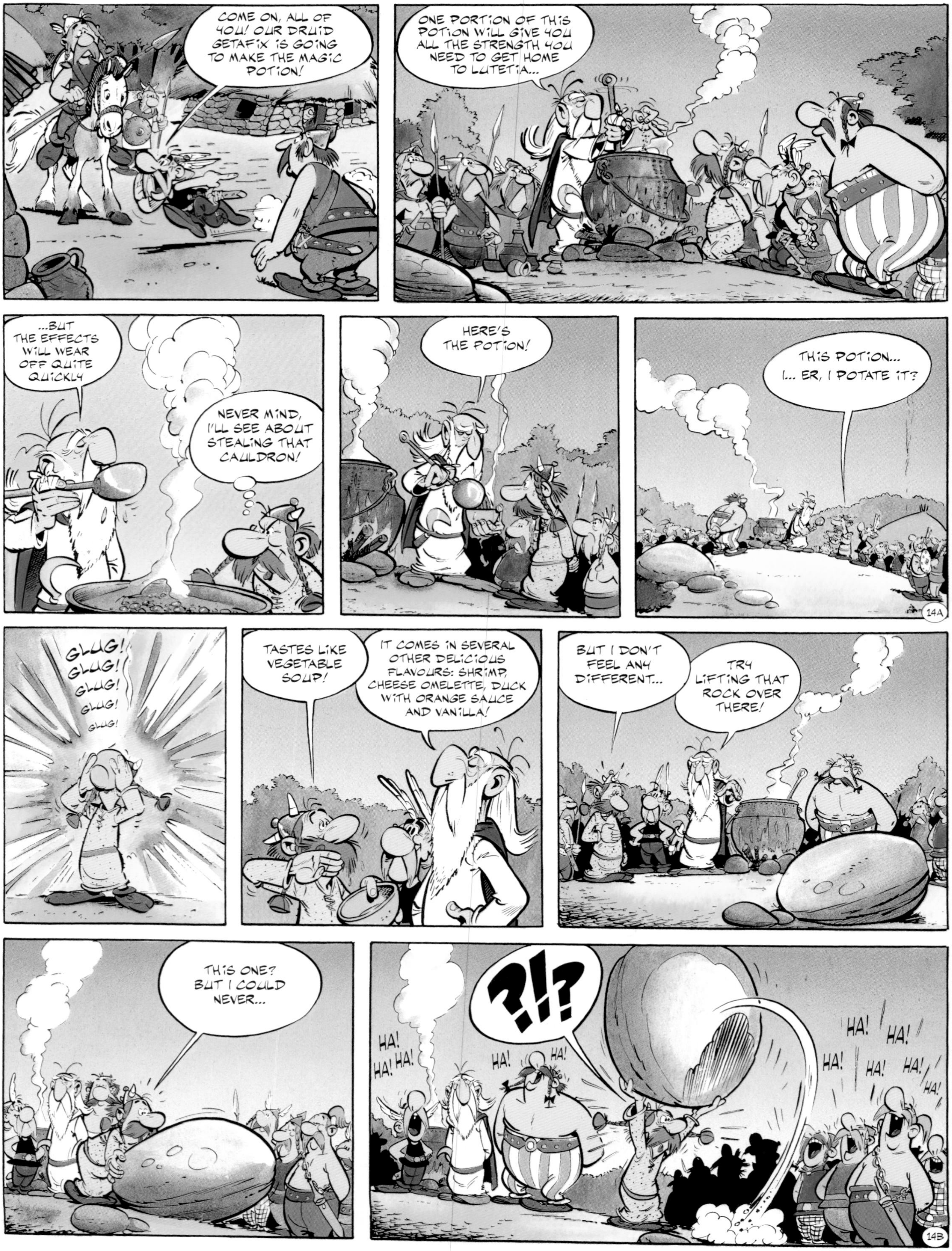

COME ON, ALL OF YOU! OUR DRUID GETAFIX IS GOING TO MAKE THE MAGIC POTION!
ONE PORTION OF THIS POTION WILL GIVE YOU ALL THE STRENGTH YOU NEED TO GET HOME TO LUTETIA...
...BUT THE EFFECTS WILL WEAR OFF QUITE QUICKLY
NEVER MIND, I'LL SEE ABOUT STEALING THAT CAULDRON!
HERE'S THE POTION!
THIS POTION... I... ER, I POTATE IT?
14A
GLUG! GLUG! GLUG! GLUG! GLUG!
TASTES LIKE VEGETABLE SOUP!
IT COMES IN SEVERAL OTHER DELICIOUS FLAVOURS: SHRIMP, CHEESE OMELETTE, DUCK WITH ORANGE SAUCE AND VANILLA!
BUT I DON'T FEEL ANY DIFFERENT...
TRY LIFTING THAT ROCK OVER THERE!
THIS ONE? BUT I COULD NEVER...
?!?
HA! HA! HA! HA! HA!
HA! HA! HA! HA! HA! HA! HA!
14B

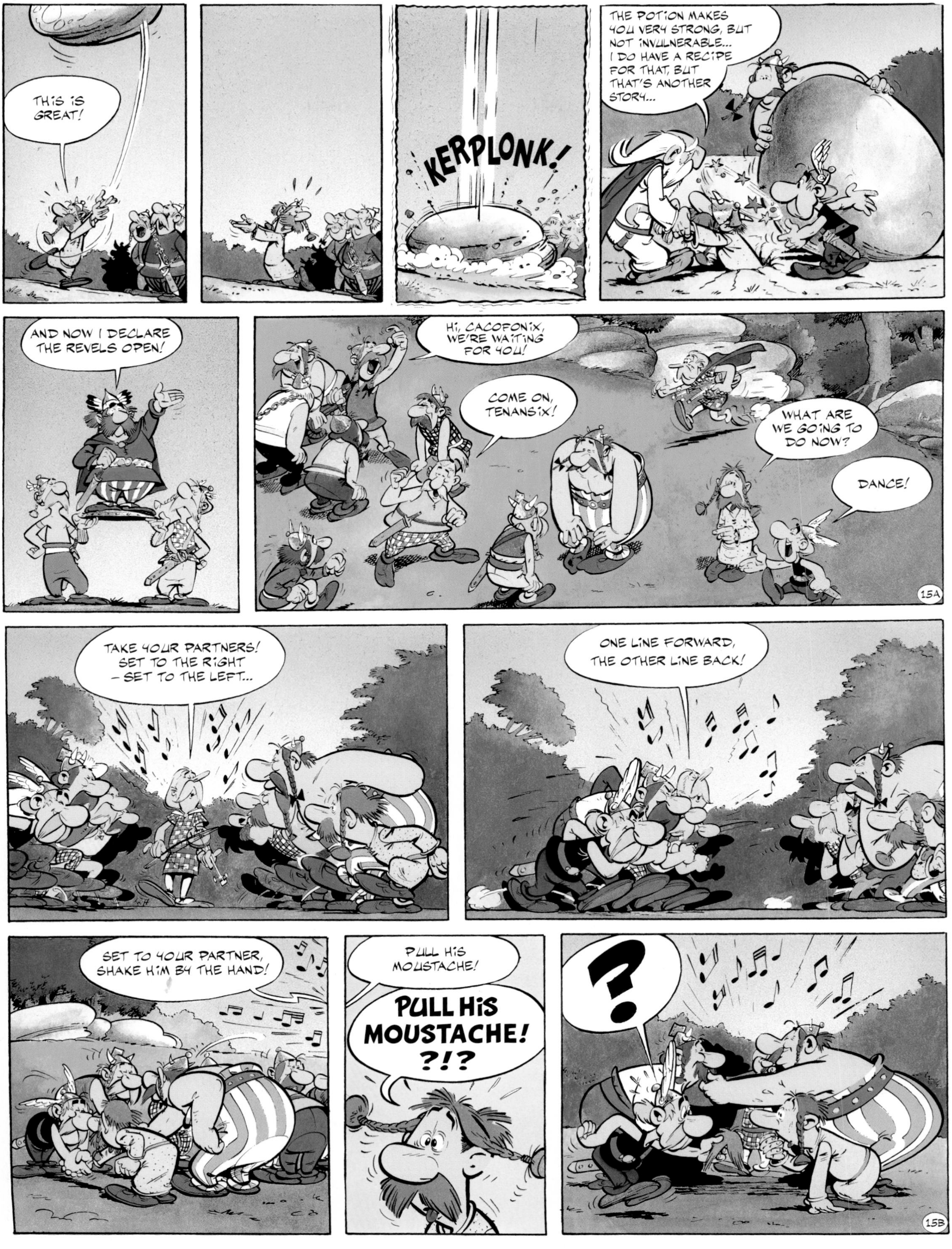
THIS IS GREAT!
KERPLONK!
THE POTION MAKES YOU VERY STRONG, BUT NOT INVULNERABLE... I DO HAVE A RECIPE FOR THAT, BUT THAT'S ANOTHER STORY...
AND NOW I DECLARE THE REVELS OPEN!
HI, CACOFONIX, WE'RE WAITING FOR YOU!
COME ON, TENANSIX!
WHAT ARE WE GOING TO DO NOW?
DANCE!
15A
TAKE YOUR PARTNERS! SET TO THE RIGHT – SET TO THE LEFT...
ONE LINE FORWARD, THE OTHER LINE BACK!
SET TO YOUR PARTNER, SHAKE HIM BY THE HAND!
PULL HIS MOUSTACHE!
PULL HIS MOUSTACHE! ?!?
?
15B

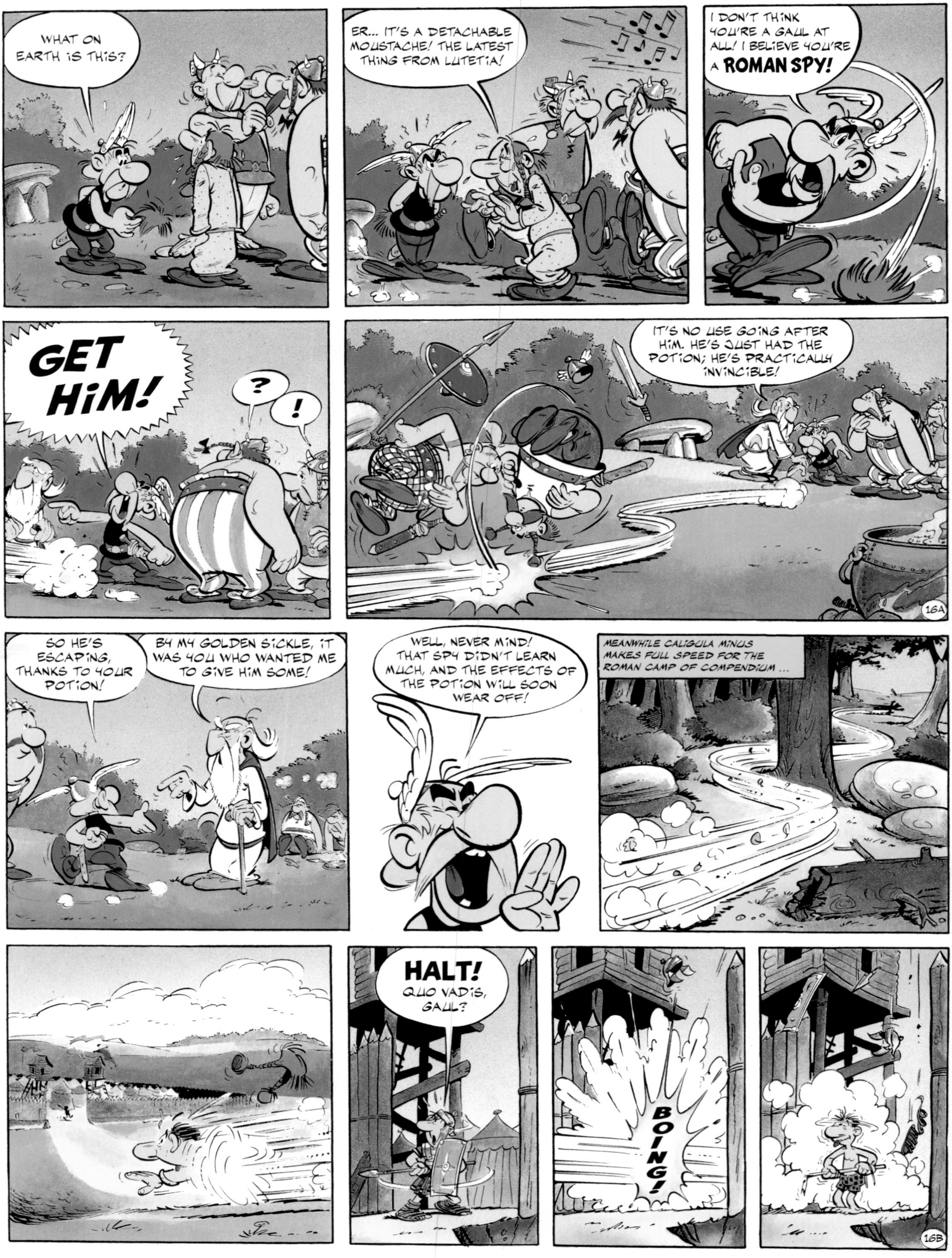
WHAT ON EARTH IS THIS?
ER... IT'S A DETACHABLE MOUSTACHE! THE LATEST THING FROM LUTETIA!
I DON'T THINK YOU'RE A GAUL AT ALL! I BELIEVE YOU'RE A ROMAN SPY!
GET HIM!
?
!
IT'S NO USE GOING AFTER HIM. HE'S JUST HAD THE POTION; HE'S PRACTICALLY INVINCIBLE!
16A
SO HE'S ESCAPING, THANKS TO YOUR POTION!
BY MY GOLDEN SICKLE, IT WAS YOU WHO WANTED ME TO GIVE HIM SOME!
WELL, NEVER MIND! THAT SPY DIDN'T LEARN MUCH, AND THE EFFECTS OF THE POTION WILL SOON WEAR OFF!
MEANWHILE CALIGULA MINUS MAKES FULL SPEED FOR THE ROMAN CAMP OF COMPENDIUM ...
HALT! QUO VADIS, GAUL?
BOING!
16B

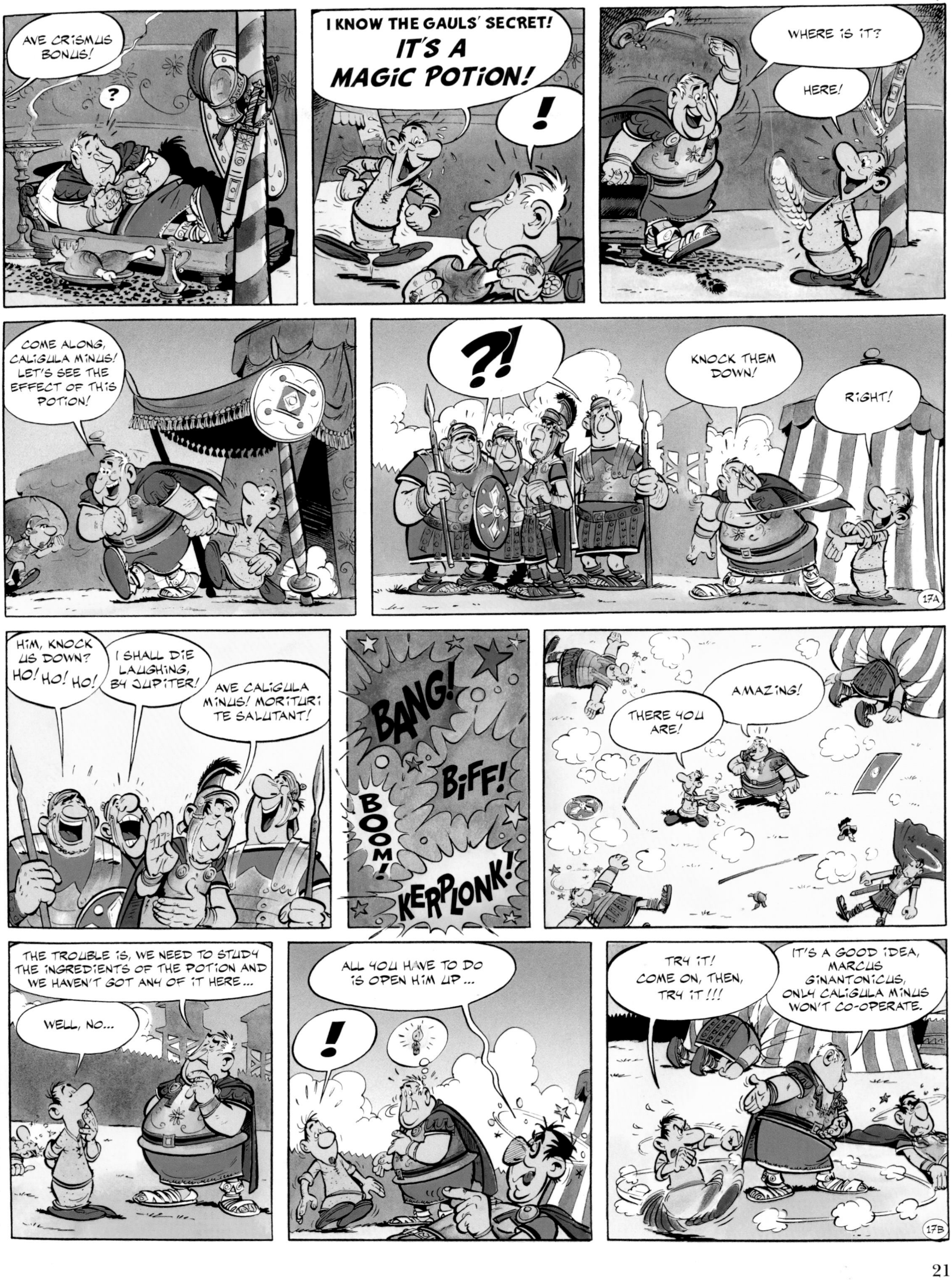
AVE CRISMUS BONUS!
?
I KNOW THE GAULS' SECRET! IT'S A MAGIC POTION!
!
WHERE IS IT?
HERE!
COME ALONG, CALIGULA MINUS! LET'S SEE THE EFFECT OF THIS POTION!
?!
KNOCK THEM DOWN!
RIGHT!
17A
HIM, KNOCK US DOWN? HO! HO! HO!
I SHALL DIE LAUGHING, BY JUPITER!
AVE CALIGULA MINUS! MORITURI TE SALUTANT!
BANG!
BIFF!
BOOM!
KERPLONK!
AMAZING!
THERE YOU ARE!
THE TROUBLE IS, WE NEED TO STUDY THE INGREDIENTS OF THE POTION AND WE HAVEN'T GOT ANY OF IT HERE...
WELL, NO...
ALL YOU HAVE TO DO IS OPEN HIM UP...
!
TRY IT! COME ON, THEN, TRY IT!!!
IT'S A GOOD IDEA, MARCUS GINANTONICUS, ONLY CALIGULA MINUS WON'T CO-OPERATE.
17B

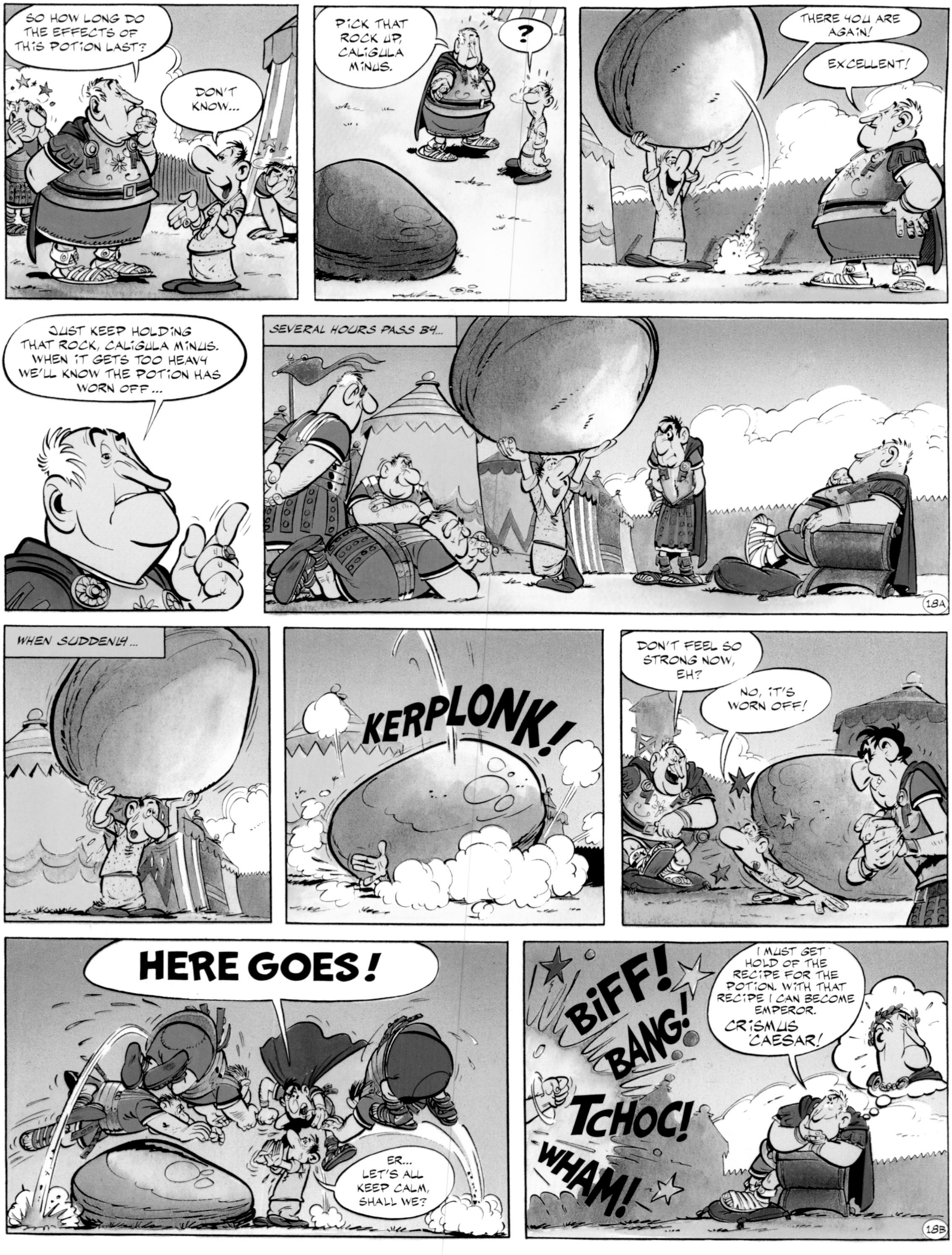
SO HOW LONG DO THE EFFECTS OF THIS POTION LAST?
DON'T KNOW...
PICK THAT ROCK UP, CALIGULA MINUS.
?
THERE YOU ARE AGAIN!
EXCELLENT!
JUST KEEP HOLDING THAT ROCK, CALIGULA MINUS. WHEN IT GETS TOO HEAVY WE'LL KNOW THE POTION HAS WORN OFF...
SEVERAL HOURS PASS BY...
WHEN SUDDENLY...
KERPLONK!
DON'T FEEL SO STRONG NOW, EH?
NO, IT'S WORN OFF!
HERE GOES!
ER... LET'S ALL KEEP CALM, SHALL WE?
BIFF!
BANG!
TCHOC!
WHAM!
I MUST GET HOLD OF THE RECIPE FOR THE POTION. WITH THAT RECIPE I CAN BECOME EMPEROR.
CRISMUS CAESAR!

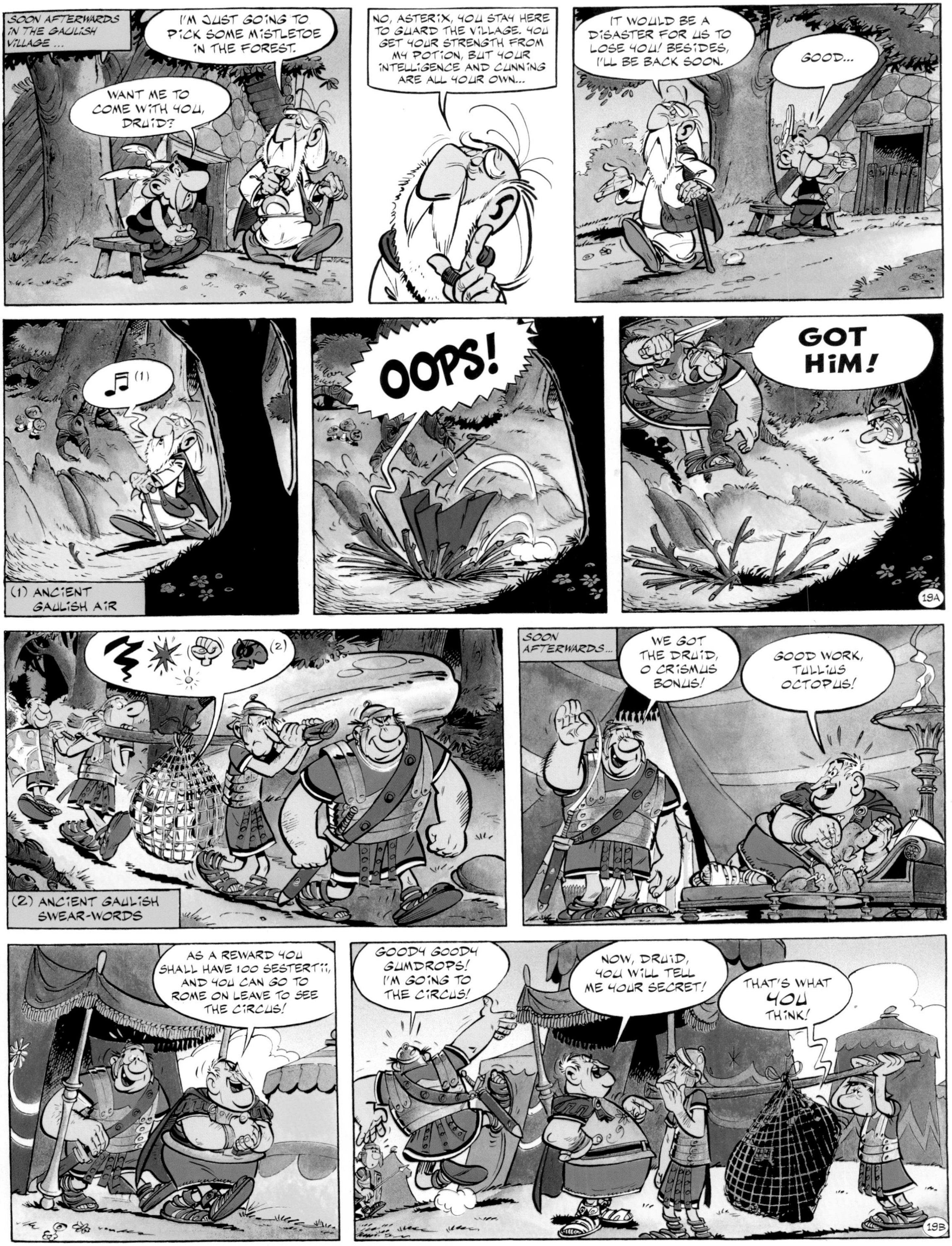

SOON AFTERWARDS IN THE GAULISH VILLAGE ...
I'M JUST GOING TO PICK SOME MISTLETOE IN THE FOREST.
WANT ME TO COME WITH YOU, DRUID?
NO, ASTERIX, YOU STAY HERE TO GUARD THE VILLAGE. YOU GET YOUR STRENGTH FROM MY POTION, BUT YOUR INTELLIGENCE AND CUNNING ARE ALL YOUR OWN...
IT WOULD BE A DISASTER FOR US TO LOSE YOU! BESIDES, I'LL BE BACK SOON.
GOOD...
(1)
(1) ANCIENT GAULISH AIR
OOPS!
GOT HIM!
19A
(2)
(2) ANCIENT GAULISH SWEAR-WORDS
SOON AFTERWARDS...
WE GOT THE DRUID, O CRISMUS BONUS!
GOOD WORK, TULLIUS OCTOPUS!
AS A REWARD YOU SHALL HAVE 100 SESTERTII, AND YOU CAN GO TO ROME ON LEAVE TO SEE THE CIRCUS!
GOODY GOODY GUMDROPS! I'M GOING TO THE CIRCUS!
NOW, DRUID, YOU WILL TELL ME YOUR SECRET!
THAT'S WHAT YOU THINK!
19B

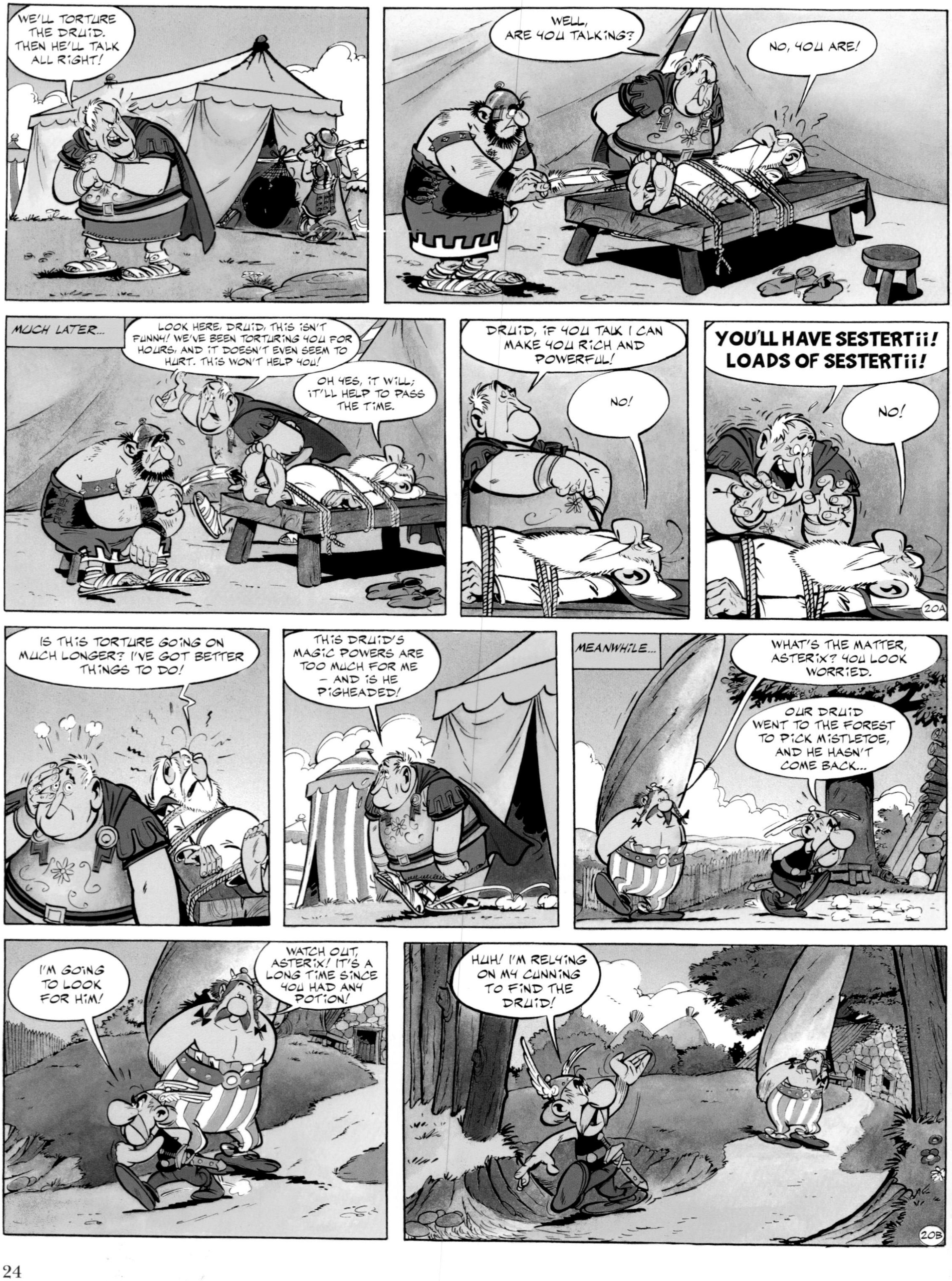

WE'LL TORTURE THE DRUID. THEN HE'LL TALK ALL RIGHT!
WELL, ARE YOU TALKING?
NO, YOU ARE!
MUCH LATER...
LOOK HERE, DRUID, THIS ISN'T FUNNY! WE'VE BEEN TORTURING YOU FOR HOURS, AND IT DOESN'T EVEN SEEM TO HURT. THIS WON'T HELP YOU!
OH YES, IT WILL; IT'LL HELP TO PASS THE TIME.
DRUID, IF YOU TALK I CAN MAKE YOU RICH AND POWERFUL!
NO!
YOU'LL HAVE SESTERTII! LOADS OF SESTERTII!
NO!
20A
IS THIS TORTURE GOING ON MUCH LONGER? I'VE GOT BETTER THINGS TO DO!
THIS DRUID'S MAGIC POWERS ARE TOO MUCH FOR ME – AND IS HE PIGHEADED!
MEANWHILE...
WHAT'S THE MATTER, ASTERIX? YOU LOOK WORRIED.
OUR DRUID WENT TO THE FOREST TO PICK MISTLETOE, AND HE HASN'T COME BACK...
I'M GOING TO LOOK FOR HIM!
WATCH OUT, ASTERIX! IT'S A LONG TIME SINCE YOU HAD ANY POTION!
HUH! I'M RELYING ON MY CUNNING TO FIND THE DRUID!
20B

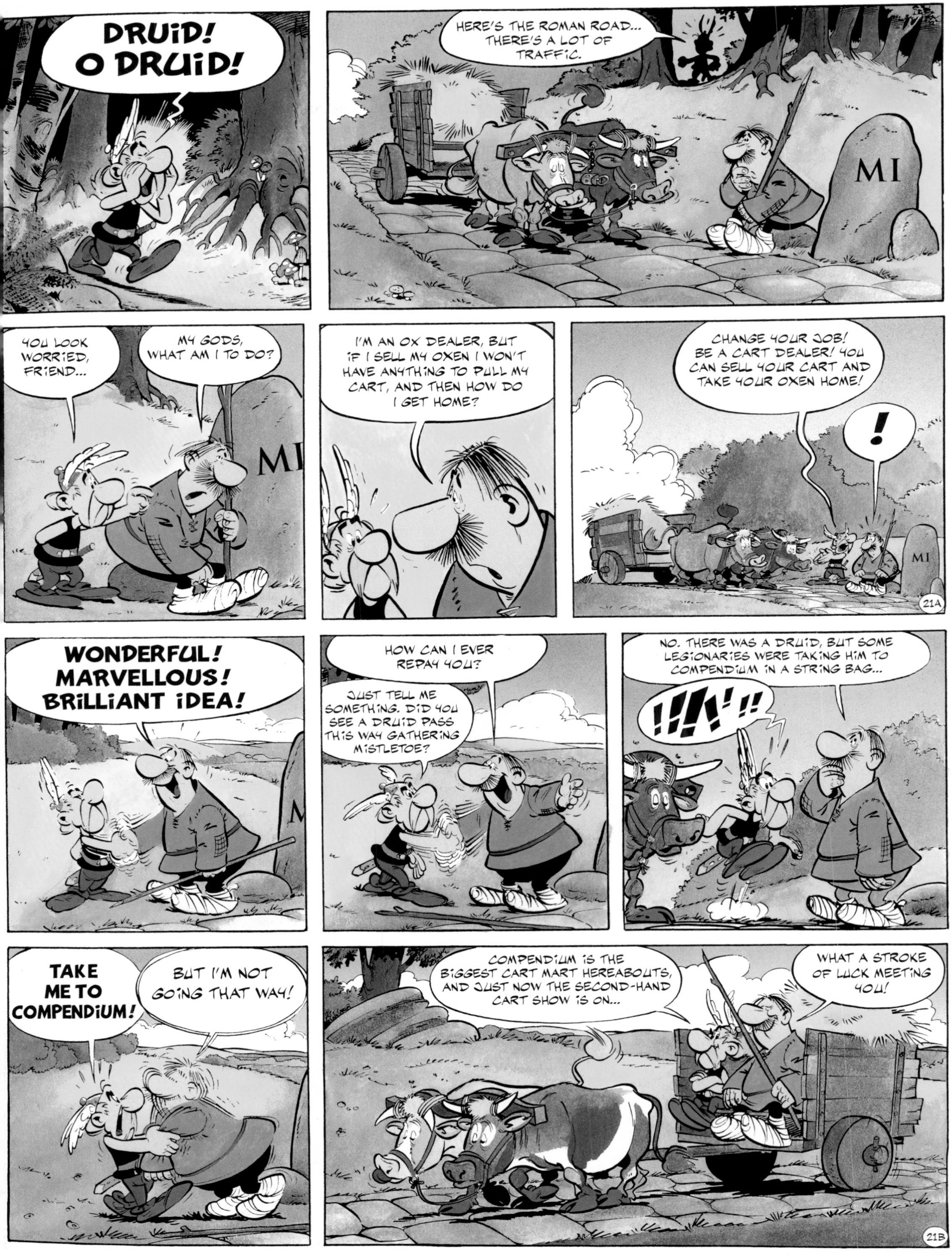
DRUID! O DRUID!
HERE'S THE ROMAN ROAD... THERE'S A LOT OF TRAFFIC.
MI
YOU LOOK WORRIED, FRIEND...
MY GODS, WHAT AM I TO DO?
MI
I'M AN OX DEALER, BUT IF I SELL MY OXEN I WON'T HAVE ANYTHING TO PULL MY CART, AND THEN HOW DO I GET HOME?
CHANGE YOUR JOB! BE A CART DEALER! YOU CAN SELL YOUR CART AND TAKE YOUR OXEN HOME!
!
MI
21A
WONDERFUL! MARVELLOUS! BRILLIANT IDEA!
HOW CAN I EVER REPAY YOU?
JUST TELL ME SOMETHING. DID YOU SEE A DRUID PASS THIS WAY GATHERING MISTLETOE?
NO. THERE WAS A DRUID, BUT SOME LEGIONARIES WERE TAKING HIM TO COMPENDIUM IN A STRING BAG...
TAKE ME TO COMPENDIUM!
BUT I'M NOT GOING THAT WAY!
COMPENDIUM IS THE BIGGEST CART MART HEREABOUTS, AND JUST NOW THE SECOND-HAND CART SHOW IS ON...
WHAT A STROKE OF LUCK MEETING YOU!
21B

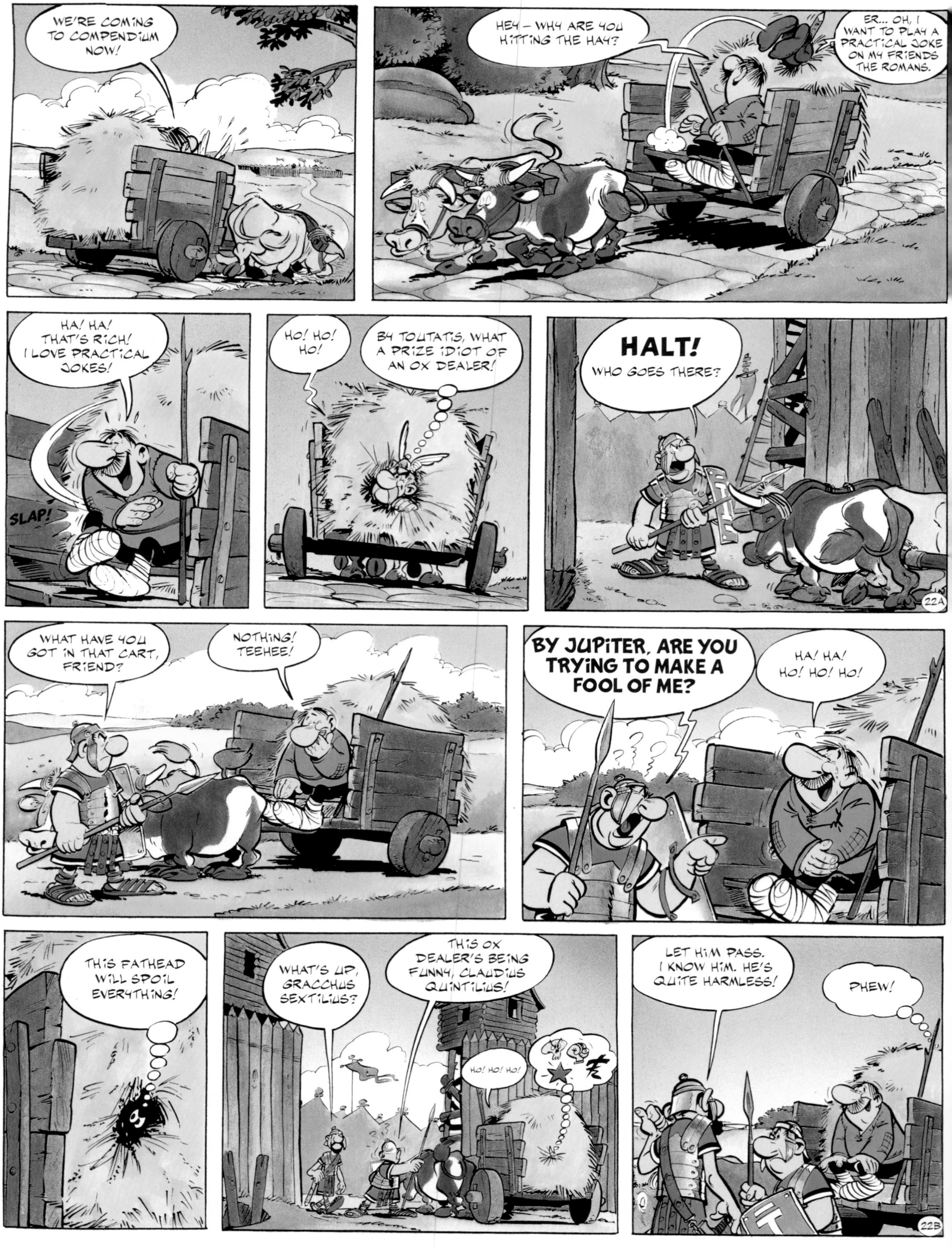
WE'RE COMING TO COMPENDIUM NOW!
HEY – WHY ARE YOU HITTING THE HAY?
ER... OH, I WANT TO PLAY A PRACTICAL JOKE ON MY FRIENDS THE ROMANS.
HA! HA! THAT'S RICH! I LOVE PRACTICAL JOKES!
SLAP!
HO! HO! HO!
BY TOUTATIS, WHAT A PRIZE IDIOT OF AN OX DEALER!
HALT!
WHO GOES THERE?
22A
WHAT HAVE YOU GOT IN THAT CART, FRIEND?
NOTHING! TEEHEE!
BY JUPITER, ARE YOU TRYING TO MAKE A FOOL OF ME?
HA! HA! HO! HO! HO!
THIS FATHEAD WILL SPOIL EVERYTHING!
WHAT'S UP, GRACCHUS SEXTILIUS?
THIS OX DEALER'S BEING FUNNY, CLAUDIUS QUINTILIUS!
HO! HO! HO!
LET HIM PASS. I KNOW HIM. HE'S QUITE HARMLESS!
PHEW!
22B

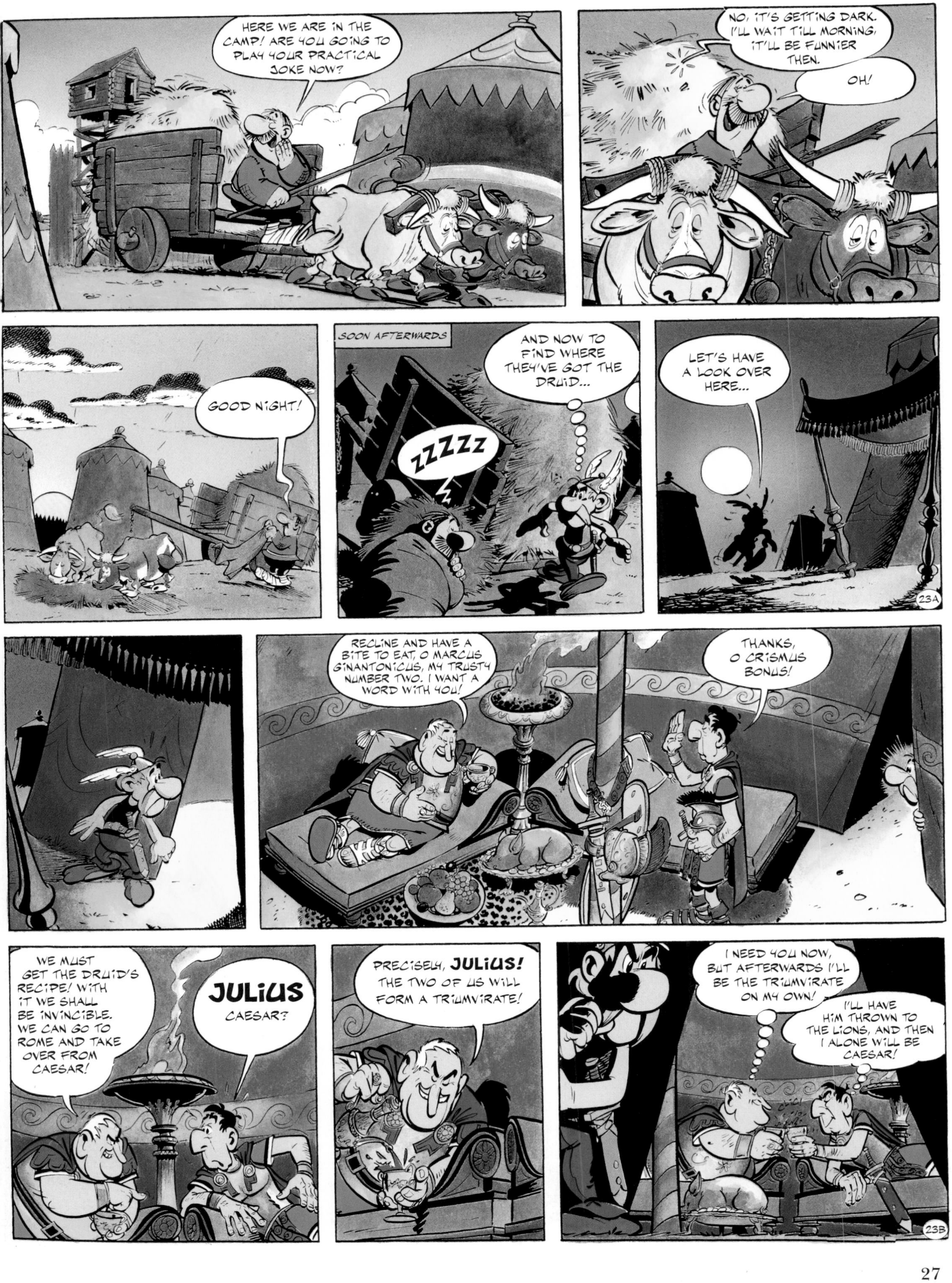
HERE WE ARE IN THE CAMP! ARE YOU GOING TO PLAY YOUR PRACTICAL JOKE NOW?
NO, IT'S GETTING DARK. I'LL WAIT TILL MORNING, IT'LL BE FUNNIER THEN.
OH!
GOOD NIGHT!
SOON AFTERWARDS
AND NOW TO FIND WHERE THEY'VE GOT THE DRUID...
ZZZZZ
LET'S HAVE A LOOK OVER HERE...
23A
RECLINE AND HAVE A BITE TO EAT, O MARCUS GINANTONICUS, MY TRUSTY NUMBER TWO. I WANT A WORD WITH YOU!
THANKS, O CRISMUS BONUS!
WE MUST GET THE DRUID'S RECIPE! WITH IT WE SHALL BE INVINCIBLE. WE CAN GO TO ROME AND TAKE OVER FROM CAESAR!
JULIUS CAESAR?
PRECISELY, JULIUS! THE TWO OF US WILL FORM A TRIUMVIRATE!
I NEED YOU NOW, BUT AFTERWARDS I'LL BE THE TRIUMVIRATE ON MY OWN!
I'LL HAVE HIM THROWN TO THE LIONS, AND THEN I ALONE WILL BE CAESAR!
23B

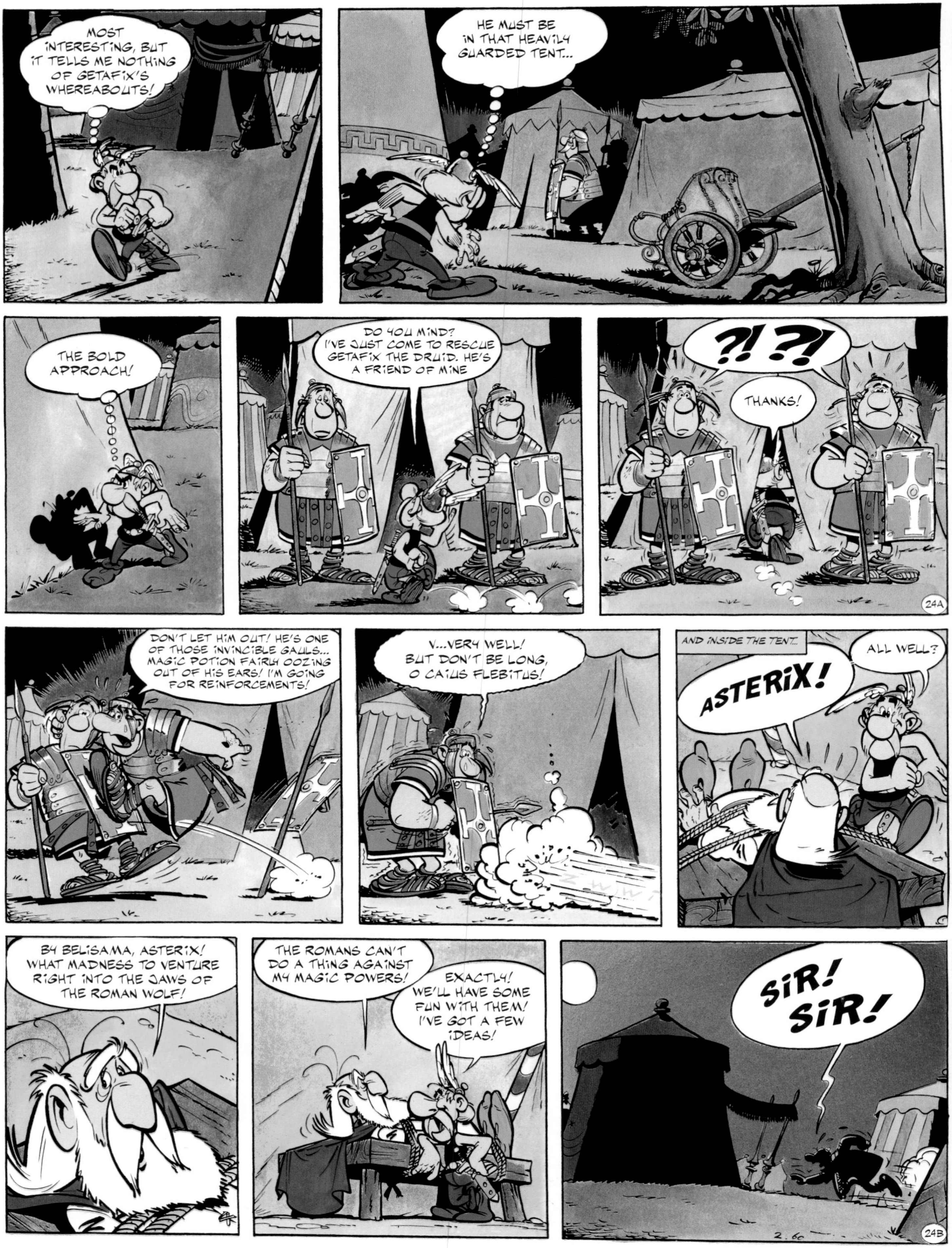

MOST INTERESTING, BUT IT TELLS ME NOTHING OF GETAFIX'S WHEREABOUTS!
HE MUST BE IN THAT HEAVILY GUARDED TENT...
THE BOLD APPROACH!
DO YOU MIND? I'VE JUST COME TO RESCUE GETAFIX THE DRUID. HE'S A FRIEND OF MINE
?! ?!
THANKS!
24A
DON'T LET HIM OUT! HE'S ONE OF THOSE INVINCIBLE GAULS... MAGIC POTION FAIRLY OOZING OUT OF HIS EARS! I'M GOING FOR REINFORCEMENTS!
V...VERY WELL! BUT DON'T BE LONG, O CAIUS FLEBITUS!
AND INSIDE THE TENT...
ASTERIX!
ALL WELL?
BY BELISAMA, ASTERIX! WHAT MADNESS TO VENTURE RIGHT INTO THE JAWS OF THE ROMAN WOLF!
THE ROMANS CAN'T DO A THING AGAINST MY MAGIC POWERS!
EXACTLY! WE'LL HAVE SOME FUN WITH THEM! I'VE GOT A FEW IDEAS!
SIR! SIR!
24B

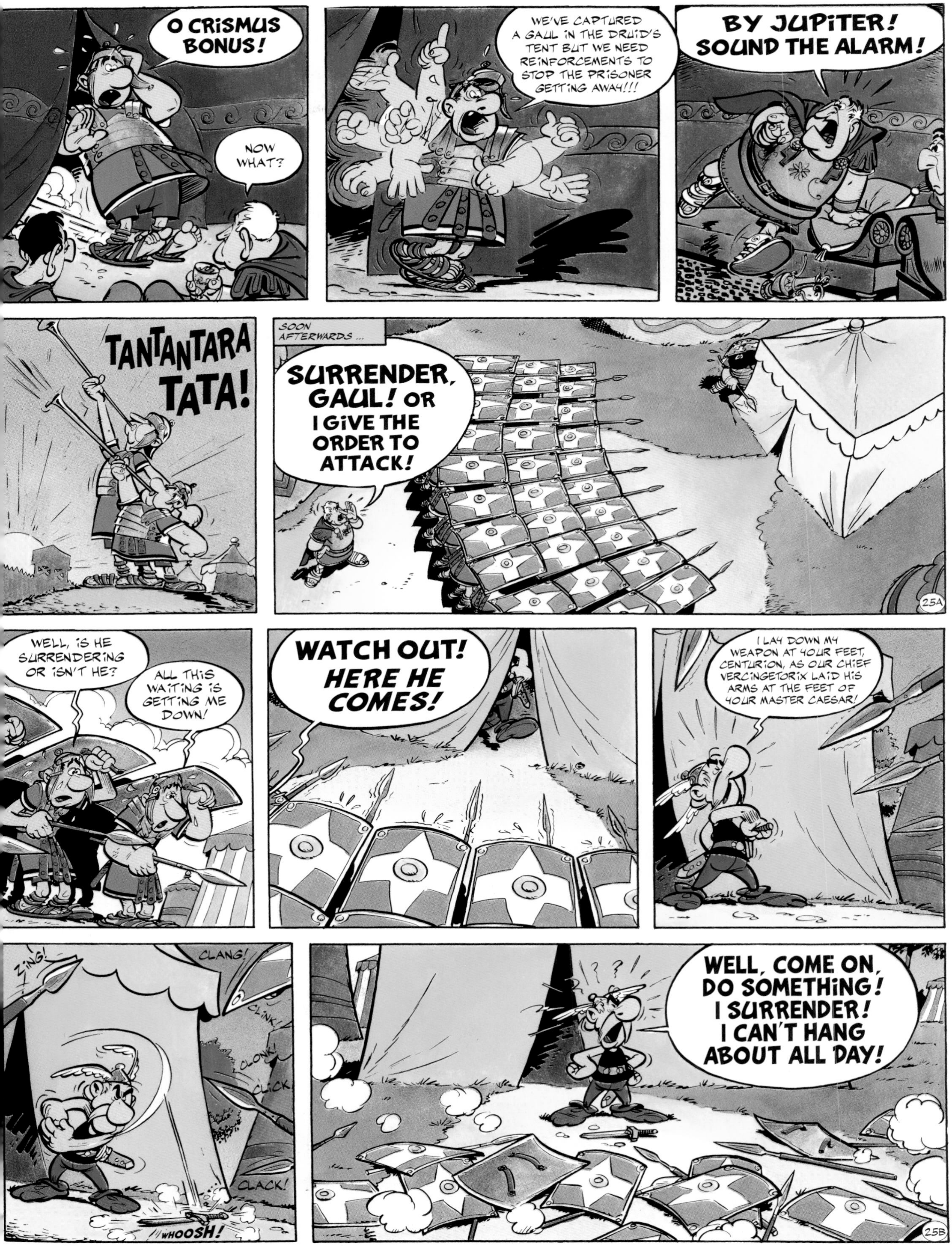
O CRISMUS BONUS!
NOW WHAT?
WE'VE CAPTURED A GAUL IN THE DRUID'S TENT BUT WE NEED REINFORCEMENTS TO STOP THE PRISONER GETTING AWAY!!!
BY JUPITER! SOUND THE ALARM!
TANTANTARA TATA!
SOON AFTERWARDS ...
SURRENDER, GAUL! OR I GIVE THE ORDER TO ATTACK!
25A
WELL, IS HE SURRENDERING OR ISN'T HE?
ALL THIS WAITING IS GETTING ME DOWN!
WATCH OUT! HERE HE COMES!
I LAY DOWN MY WEAPON AT YOUR FEET, CENTURION, AS OUR CHIEF VERCINGETORIX LAID HIS ARMS AT THE FEET OF YOUR MASTER CAESAR!
ZING!
CLANG!
CLINK!
DLONK!
CLICK
CLACK!
WHOOSH!
WELL, COME ON, DO SOMETHING! I SURRENDER! I CAN'T HANG ABOUT ALL DAY!
25B

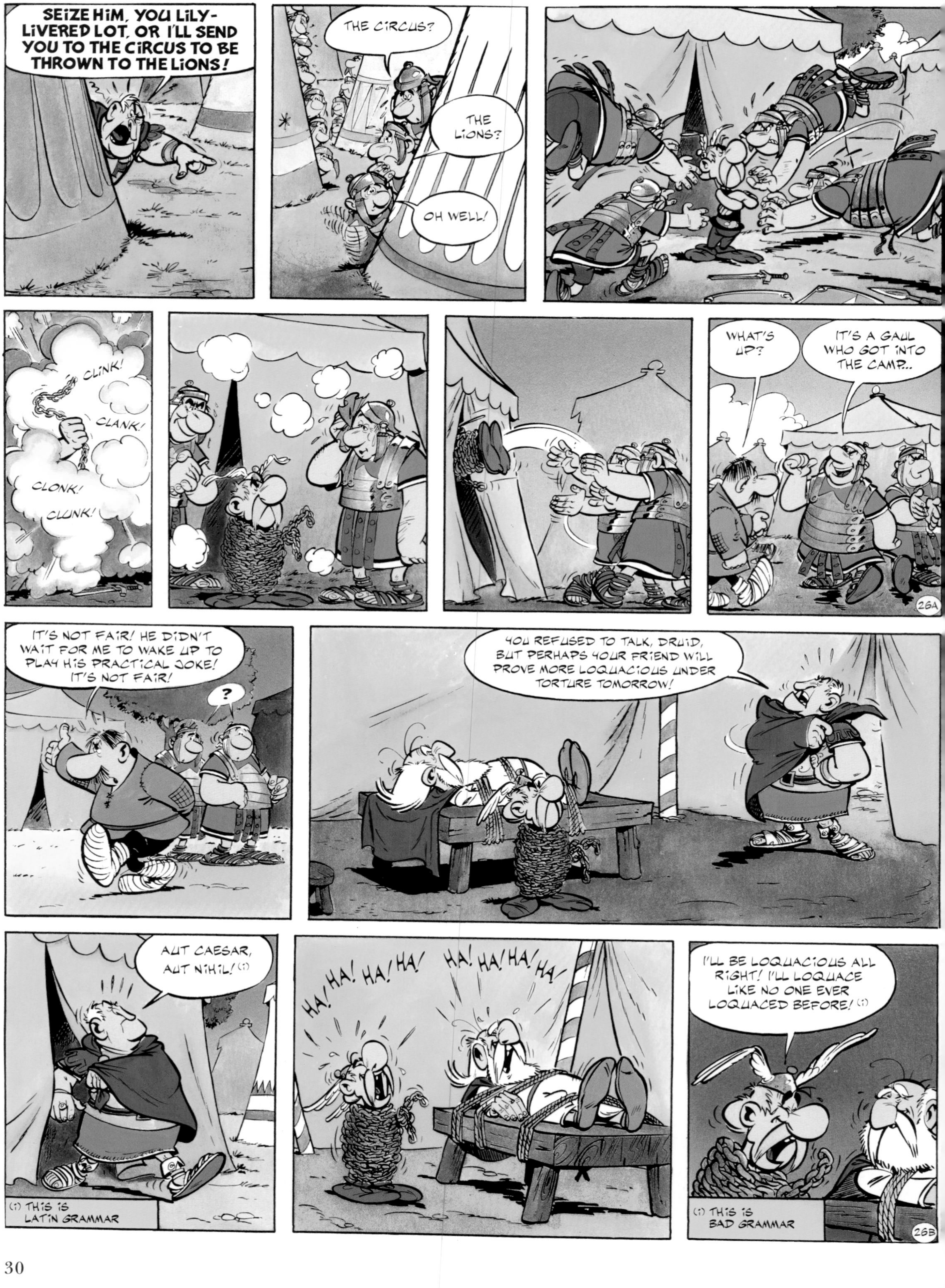
SEIZE HIM, YOU LILY-LIVERED LOT, OR I'LL SEND YOU TO THE CIRCUS TO BE THROWN TO THE LIONS!
THE CIRCUS?
THE LIONS?
OH WELL!
CLINK!
CLANK!
CLONK!
CLUNK!
WHAT'S UP?
IT'S A GAUL WHO GOT INTO THE CAMP...
26A
IT'S NOT FAIR! HE DIDN'T WAIT FOR ME TO WAKE UP TO PLAY HIS PRACTICAL JOKE! IT'S NOT FAIR!
?
YOU REFUSED TO TALK, DRUID, BUT PERHAPS YOUR FRIEND WILL PROVE MORE LOQUACIOUS UNDER TORTURE TOMORROW!
AUT CAESAR, AUT NIHIL! (1)
(1) THIS IS LATIN GRAMMAR
HA! HA! HA! HA! HA! HA! HA! HA!
I'LL BE LOQUACIOUS ALL RIGHT! I'LL LOQUACE LIKE NO ONE EVER LOQUACED BEFORE! (1)
(1) THIS IS BAD GRAMMAR
26B

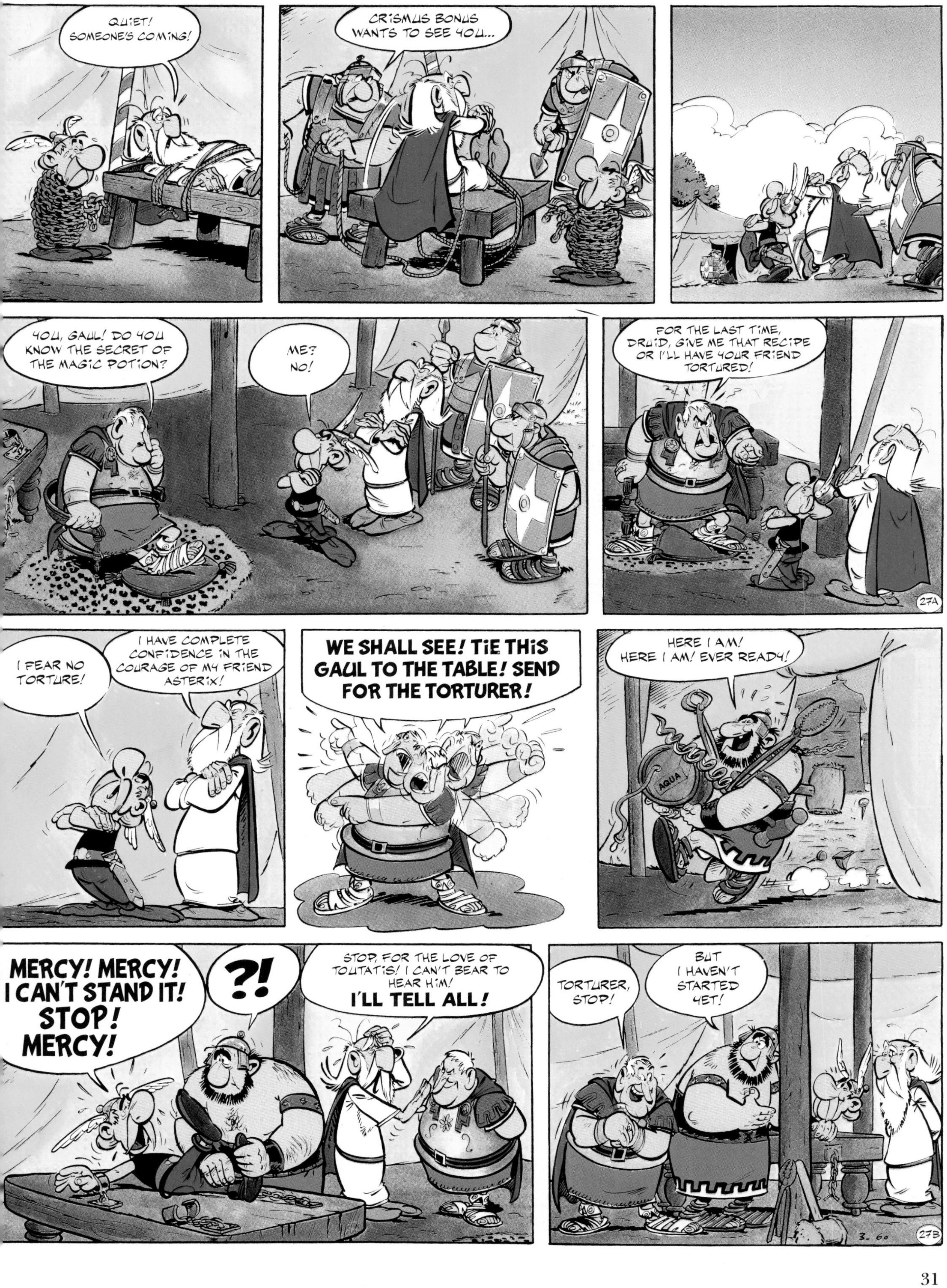
QUIET! SOMEONE'S COMING!
CRISMUS BONUS WANTS TO SEE YOU...
YOU, GAUL! DO YOU KNOW THE SECRET OF THE MAGIC POTION?
ME? NO!
FOR THE LAST TIME, DRUID, GIVE ME THAT RECIPE OR I'LL HAVE YOUR FRIEND TORTURED!
27A
I FEAR NO TORTURE!
I HAVE COMPLETE CONFIDENCE IN THE COURAGE OF MY FRIEND ASTERIX!
WE SHALL SEE! TIE THIS GAUL TO THE TABLE! SEND FOR THE TORTURER!
HERE I AM! HERE I AM! EVER READY!
AQUA
MERCY! MERCY! I CAN'T STAND IT! STOP! MERCY!
?!
STOP, FOR THE LOVE OF TOUTATIS! I CAN'T BEAR TO HEAR HIM! I'LL TELL ALL!
TORTURER, STOP!
BUT I HAVEN'T STARTED YET!
3. 60
27B

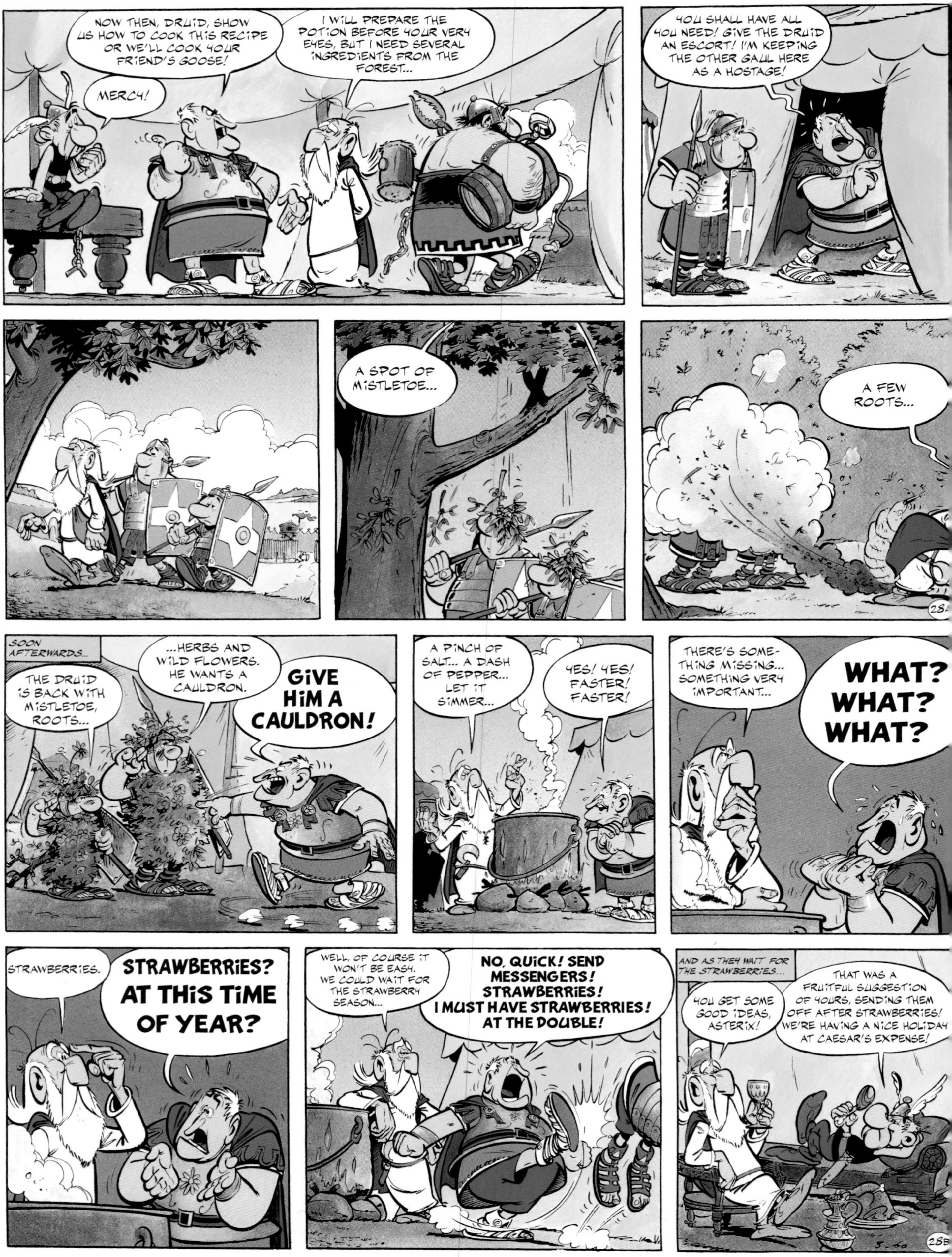
NOW THEN, DRUID, SHOW US HOW TO COOK THIS RECIPE OR WE'LL COOK YOUR FRIEND'S GOOSE!
MERCY!
I WILL PREPARE THE POTION BEFORE YOUR VERY EYES, BUT I NEED SEVERAL INGREDIENTS FROM THE FOREST...
YOU SHALL HAVE ALL YOU NEED! GIVE THE DRUID AN ESCORT! I'M KEEPING THE OTHER GAUL HERE AS A HOSTAGE!
A SPOT OF MISTLETOE...
A FEW ROOTS...
28A
SOON AFTERWARDS...
THE DRUID IS BACK WITH MISTLETOE, ROOTS...
...HERBS AND WILD FLOWERS. HE WANTS A CAULDRON.
GIVE HIM A CAULDRON!
A PINCH OF SALT... A DASH OF PEPPER... LET IT SIMMER...
YES! YES! FASTER! FASTER!
THERE'S SOMETHING MISSING... SOMETHING VERY IMPORTANT...
WHAT? WHAT? WHAT?
STRAWBERRIES.
STRAWBERRIES? AT THIS TIME OF YEAR?
WELL, OF COURSE IT WON'T BE EASY. WE COULD WAIT FOR THE STRAWBERRY SEASON...
NO, QUICK! SEND MESSENGERS! STRAWBERRIES! I MUST HAVE STRAWBERRIES! AT THE DOUBLE!
AND AS THEY WAIT FOR THE STRAWBERRIES...
YOU GET SOME GOOD IDEAS, ASTERIX!
THAT WAS A FRUITFUL SUGGESTION OF YOURS, SENDING THEM OFF AFTER STRAWBERRIES! WE'RE HAVING A NICE HOLIDAY AT CAESAR'S EXPENSE!
28B

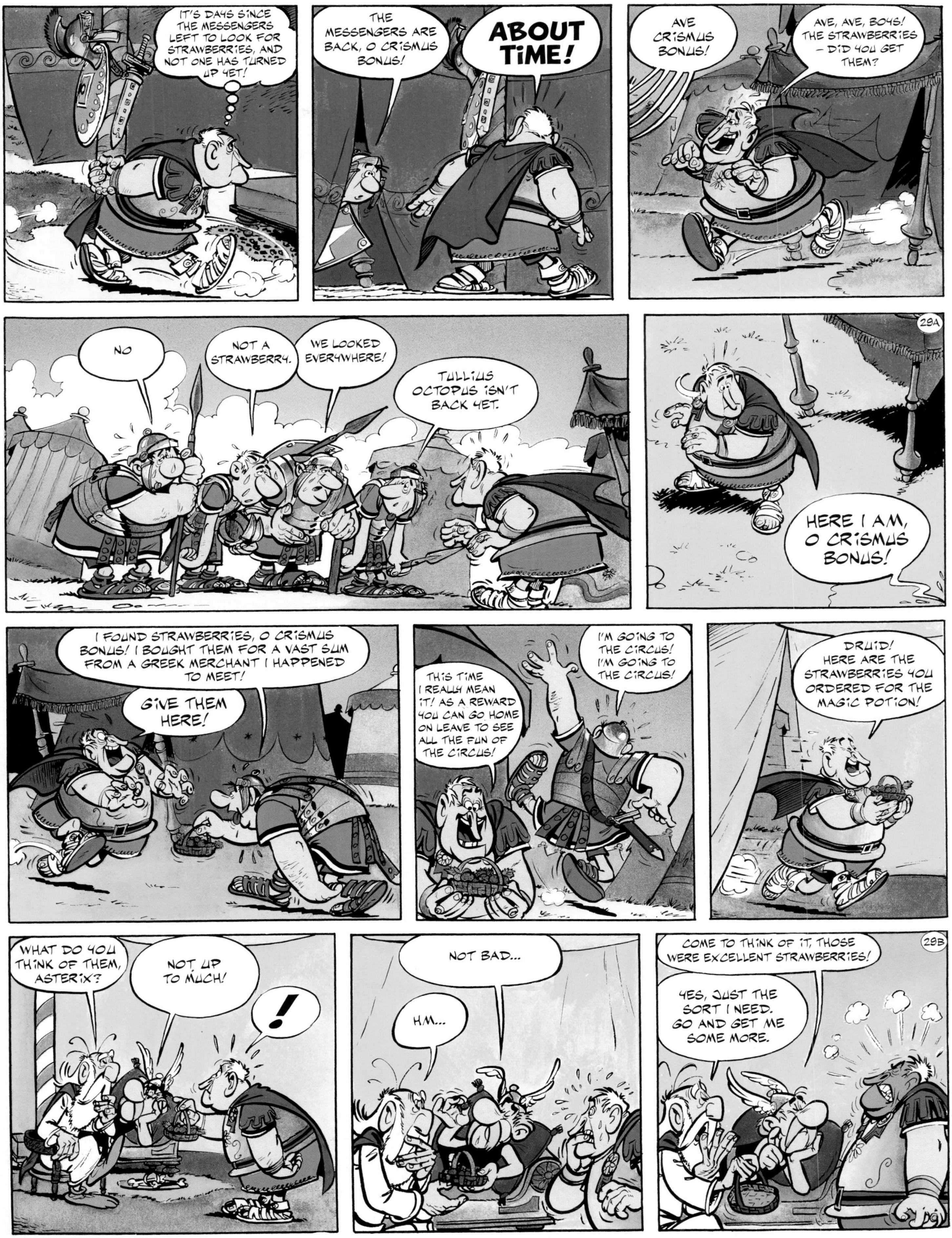
IT'S DAYS SINCE THE MESSENGERS LEFT TO LOOK FOR STRAWBERRIES, AND NOT ONE HAS TURNED UP YET!
THE MESSENGERS ARE BACK, O CRISMUS BONUS!
ABOUT TIME!
AVE CRISMUS BONUS!
AVE, AVE, BOYS! THE STRAWBERRIES – DID YOU GET THEM?
NO
NOT A STRAWBERRY.
WE LOOKED EVERYWHERE!
TULLIUS OCTOPUS ISN'T BACK YET.
29A
HERE I AM, O CRISMUS BONUS!
I FOUND STRAWBERRIES, O CRISMUS BONUS! I BOUGHT THEM FOR A VAST SUM FROM A GREEK MERCHANT I HAPPENED TO MEET!
GIVE THEM HERE!
THIS TIME I REALLY MEAN IT! AS A REWARD YOU CAN GO HOME ON LEAVE TO SEE ALL THE FUN OF THE CIRCUS!
I'M GOING TO THE CIRCUS! I'M GOING TO THE CIRCUS!
DRUID! HERE ARE THE STRAWBERRIES YOU ORDERED FOR THE MAGIC POTION!
WHAT DO YOU THINK OF THEM, ASTERIX?
NOT UP TO MUCH!
!
NOT BAD...
HM...
29B
COME TO THINK OF IT, THOSE WERE EXCELLENT STRAWBERRIES!
YES, JUST THE SORT I NEED. GO AND GET ME SOME MORE.

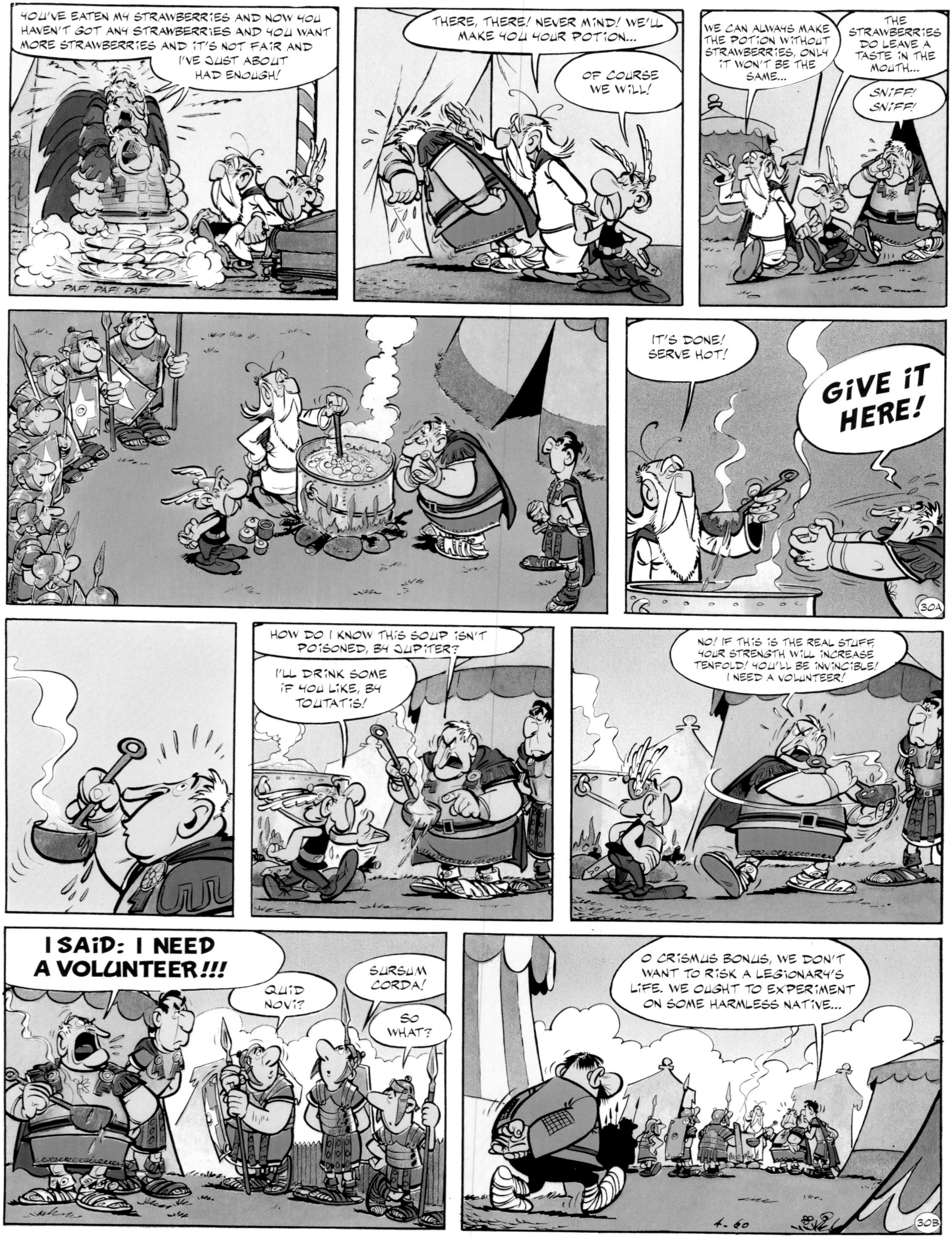
YOU'VE EATEN MY STRAWBERRIES AND NOW YOU HAVEN'T GOT ANY STRAWBERRIES AND YOU WANT MORE STRAWBERRIES AND IT'S NOT FAIR AND I'VE JUST ABOUT HAD ENOUGH!
PAF! PAF! PAF!
THERE, THERE! NEVER MIND! WE'LL MAKE YOU YOUR POTION...
OF COURSE WE WILL!
WE CAN ALWAYS MAKE THE POTION WITHOUT STRAWBERRIES, ONLY IT WON'T BE THE SAME...
THE STRAWBERRIES DO LEAVE A TASTE IN THE MOUTH...
SNIFF! SNIFF!
IT'S DONE! SERVE HOT!
GIVE IT HERE!
30A
HOW DO I KNOW THIS SOUP ISN'T POISONED, BY JUPITER?
I'LL DRINK SOME IF YOU LIKE, BY TOUTATIS!
NO! IF THIS IS THE REAL STUFF, YOUR STRENGTH WILL INCREASE TENFOLD! YOU'LL BE INVINCIBLE! I NEED A VOLUNTEER!
I SAID: I NEED A VOLUNTEER!!!
QUID NOVI?
SURSUM CORDA!
SO WHAT?
O CRISMUS BONUS, WE DON'T WANT TO RISK A LEGIONARY'S LIFE. WE OUGHT TO EXPERIMENT ON SOME HARMLESS NATIVE...
4-60
30B

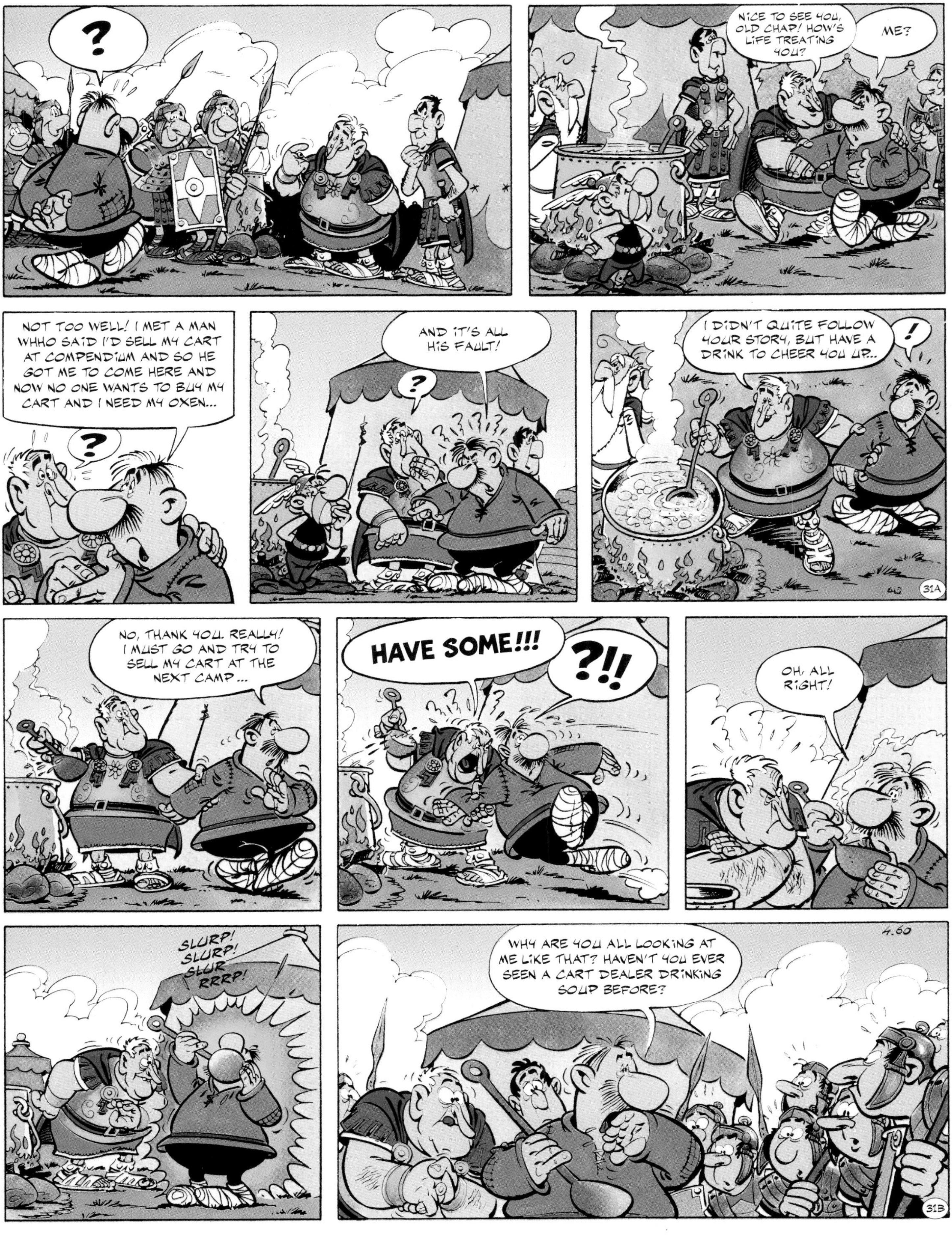
?
NICE TO SEE YOU, OLD CHAP! HOW'S LIFE TREATING YOU?
ME?
NOT TOO WELL! I MET A MAN WHHO SAID I'D SELL MY CART AT COMPENDIUM AND SO HE GOT ME TO COME HERE AND NOW NO ONE WANTS TO BUY MY CART AND I NEED MY OXEN...
?
AND IT'S ALL HIS FAULT!
?
I DIDN'T QUITE FOLLOW YOUR STORY, BUT HAVE A DRINK TO CHEER YOU UP..
!
31A
NO, THANK YOU. REALLY! I MUST GO AND TRY TO SELL MY CART AT THE NEXT CAMP...
HAVE SOME!!!
?!!
OH, ALL RIGHT!
SLURP! SLURP! SLUR RRRP!
WHY ARE YOU ALL LOOKING AT ME LIKE THAT? HAVEN'T YOU EVER SEEN A CART DEALER DRINKING SOUP BEFORE?
31B

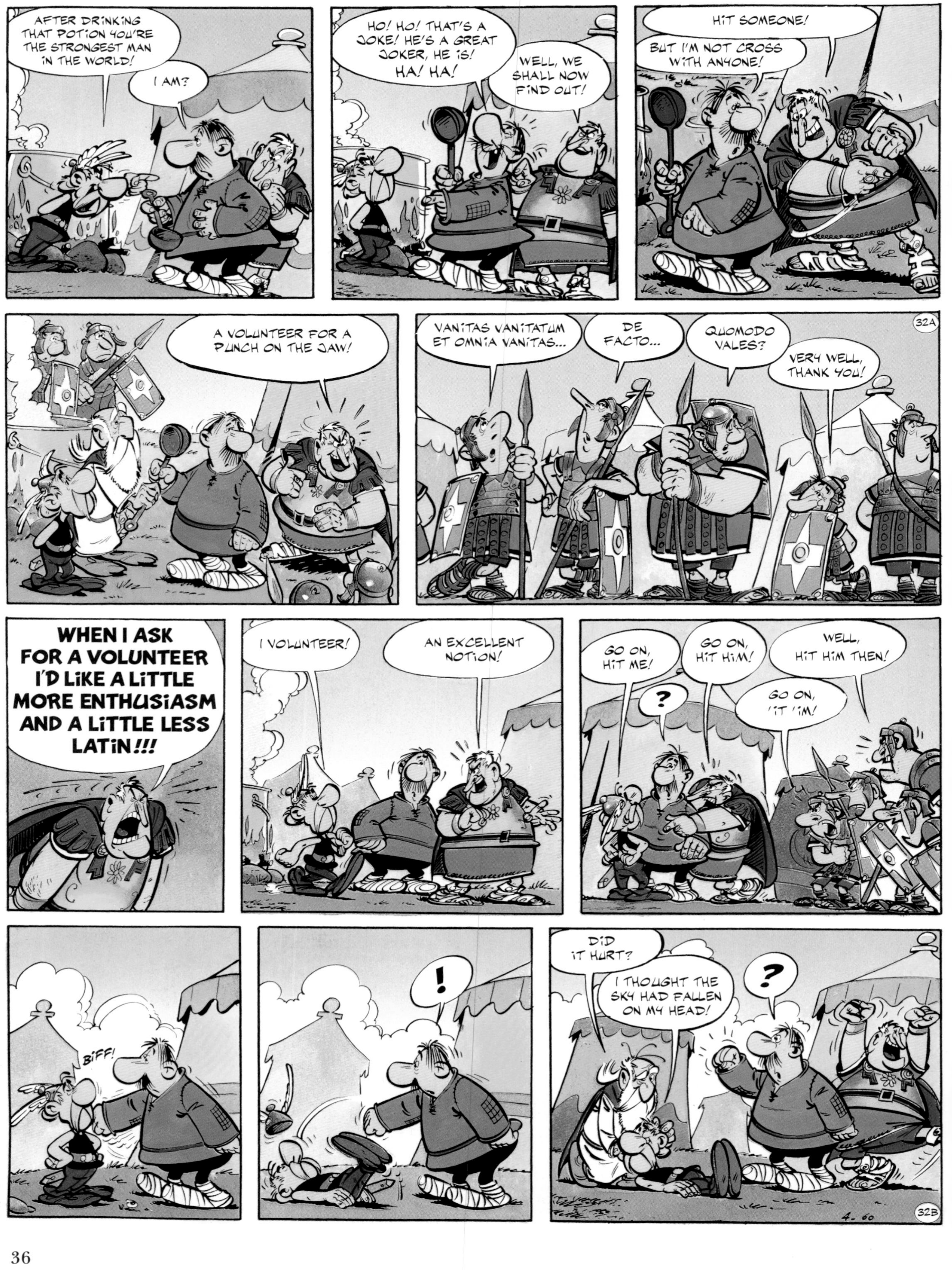
AFTER DRINKING THAT POTION YOU'RE THE STRONGEST MAN IN THE WORLD!
I AM?
HO! HO! THAT'S A JOKE! HE'S A GREAT JOKER, HE IS! HA! HA!
WELL, WE SHALL NOW FIND OUT!
HIT SOMEONE!
BUT I'M NOT CROSS WITH ANYONE!
A VOLUNTEER FOR A PUNCH ON THE JAW!
VANITAS VANITATUM ET OMNIA VANITAS...
DE FACTO...
QUOMODO VALES?
VERY WELL, THANK YOU!
32A
WHEN I ASK FOR A VOLUNTEER I'D LIKE A LITTLE MORE ENTHUSIASM AND A LITTLE LESS LATIN!!!
I VOLUNTEER!
AN EXCELLENT NOTION!
GO ON, HIT ME!
?
GO ON, HIT HIM!
WELL, HIT HIM THEN!
GO ON, 'IT 'IM!
BIFF!
!
DID IT HURT?
I THOUGHT THE SKY HAD FALLEN ON MY HEAD!
?
4. 60
32B

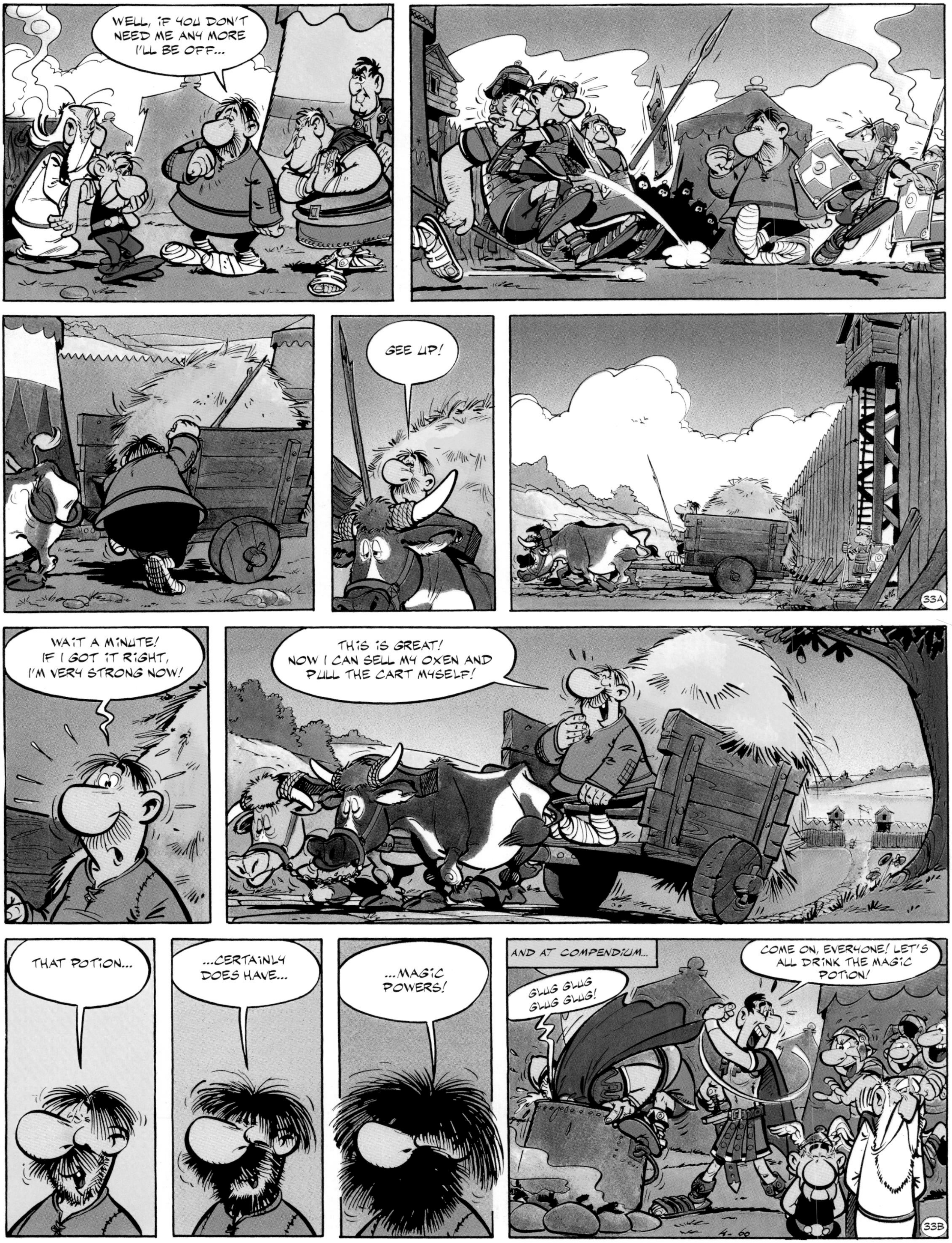
WELL, IF YOU DON'T NEED ME ANY MORE I'LL BE OFF...
GEE UP!
33A
WAIT A MINUTE! IF I GOT IT RIGHT, I'M VERY STRONG NOW!
THIS IS GREAT! NOW I CAN SELL MY OXEN AND PULL THE CART MYSELF!
THAT POTION...
...CERTAINLY DOES HAVE...
...MAGIC POWERS!
AND AT COMPENDIUM...
GLUG GLUG GLUG GLUG!
COME ON, EVERYONE! LET'S ALL DRINK THE MAGIC POTION!
33B

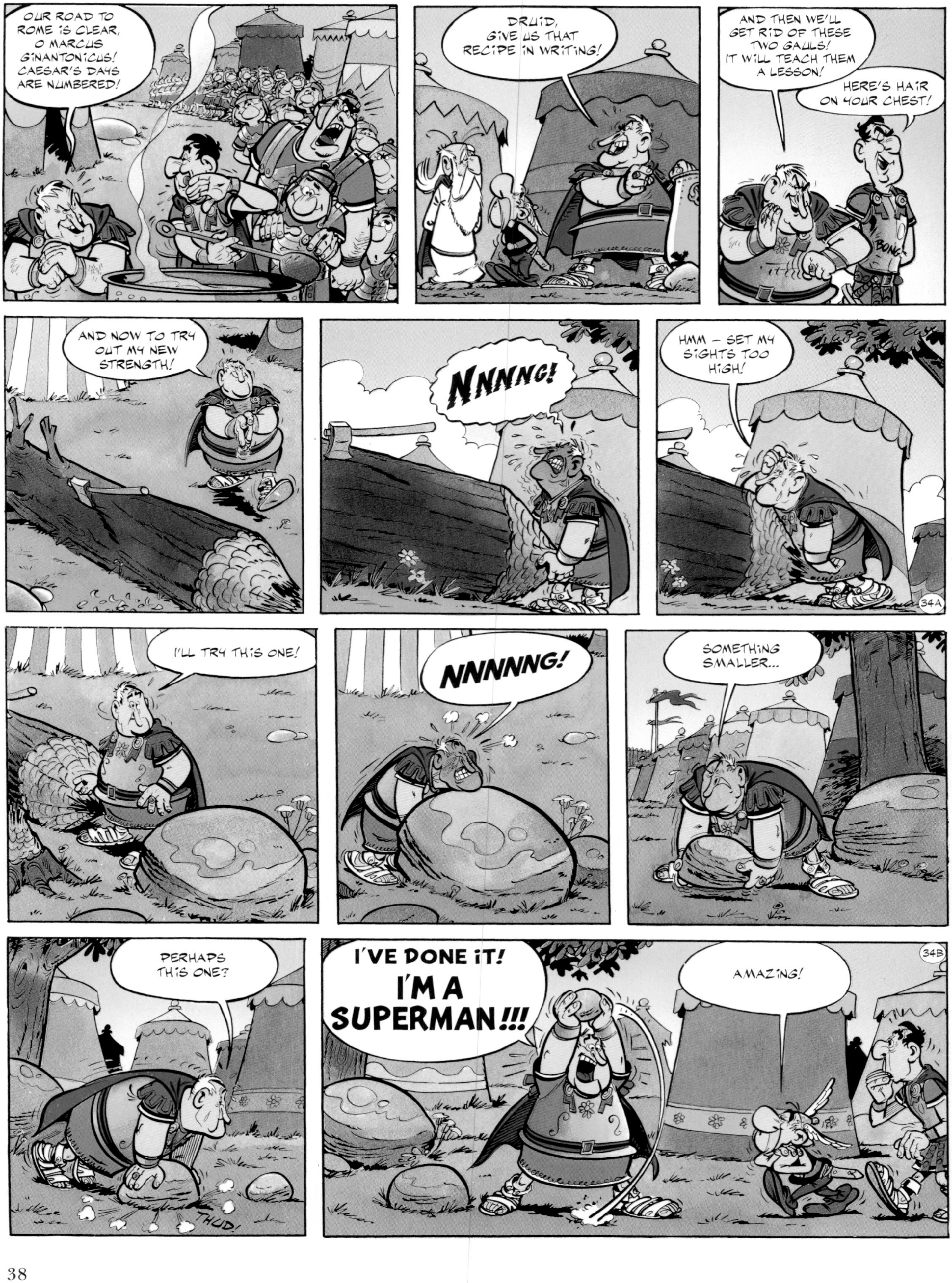
OUR ROAD TO ROME IS CLEAR, O MARCUS GINANTONICUS! CAESAR'S DAYS ARE NUMBERED!
DRUID, GIVE US THAT RECIPE IN WRITING!
AND THEN WE'LL GET RID OF THESE TWO GAULS! IT WILL TEACH THEM A LESSON!
HERE'S HAIR ON YOUR CHEST!
BONG
AND NOW TO TRY OUT MY NEW STRENGTH!
NNNNG!
HMM – SET MY SIGHTS TOO HIGH!
I'LL TRY THIS ONE!
NNNNNG!
SOMETHING SMALLER...
PERHAPS THIS ONE?
THUD!
I'VE DONE IT! I'M A SUPERMAN!!!
AMAZING!

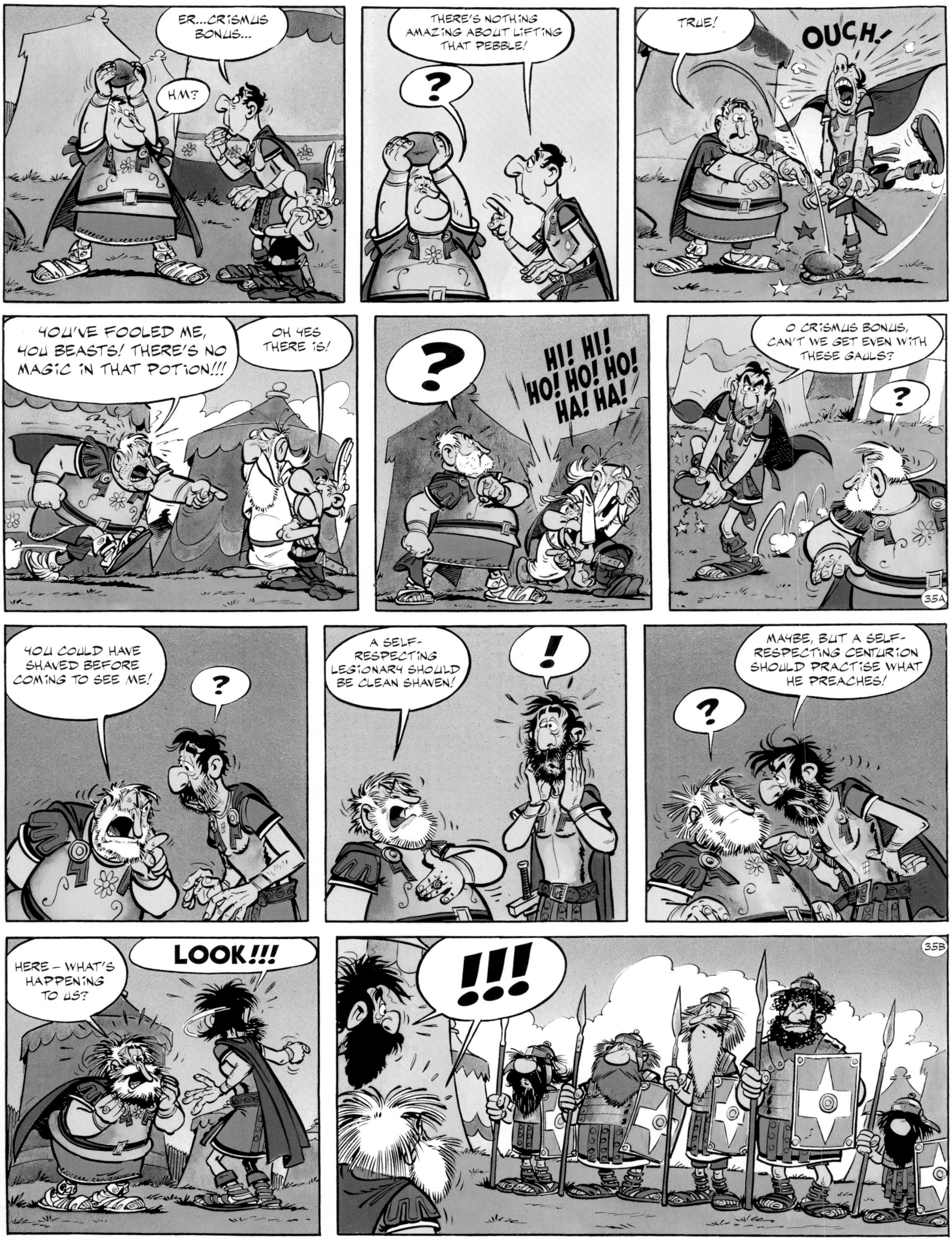

ER...CRISMUS BONUS...
HM?
THERE'S NOTHING AMAZING ABOUT LIFTING THAT PEBBLE!
?
TRUE!
OUCH!
YOU'VE FOOLED ME, YOU BEASTS! THERE'S NO MAGIC IN THAT POTION!!!
OH YES THERE IS!
?
HI! HI! HO! HO! HO! HA! HA!
O CRISMUS BONUS, CAN'T WE GET EVEN WITH THESE GAULS?
?
35A
YOU COULD HAVE SHAVED BEFORE COMING TO SEE ME!
?
A SELF-RESPECTING LEGIONARY SHOULD BE CLEAN SHAVEN!
!
MAYBE, BUT A SELF-RESPECTING CENTURION SHOULD PRACTISE WHAT HE PREACHES!
?
HERE – WHAT'S HAPPENING TO US?
LOOK!!!
35B
!!!

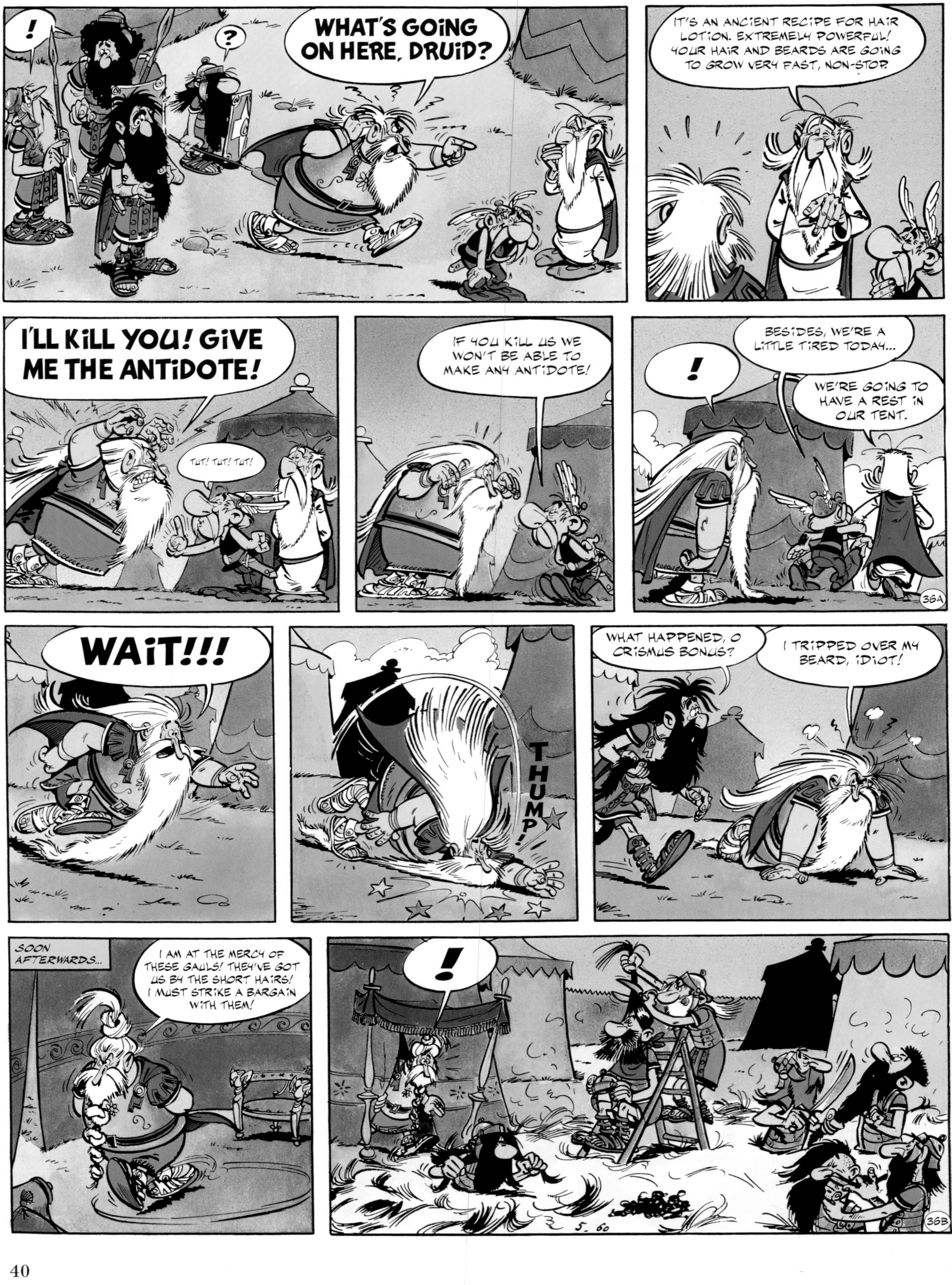
!
?
WHAT'S GOING ON HERE, DRUID?
IT'S AN ANCIENT RECIPE FOR HAIR LOTION. EXTREMELY POWERFUL! YOUR HAIR AND BEARDS ARE GOING TO GROW VERY FAST, NON-STOP.
I'LL KILL YOU! GIVE ME THE ANTIDOTE!
TUT! TUT! TUT!
IF YOU KILL US WE WON'T BE ABLE TO MAKE ANY ANTIDOTE!
!
BESIDES, WE'RE A LITTLE TIRED TODAY...
WE'RE GOING TO HAVE A REST IN OUR TENT.
36A
WAIT!!!
THUMP!
WHAT HAPPENED, O CRISMUS BONUS?
I TRIPPED OVER MY BEARD, IDIOT!
SOON AFTERWARDS...
I AM AT THE MERCY OF THESE GAULS! THEY'VE GOT US BY THE SHORT HAIRS! I MUST STRIKE A BARGAIN WITH THEM!
!
5.60
36B

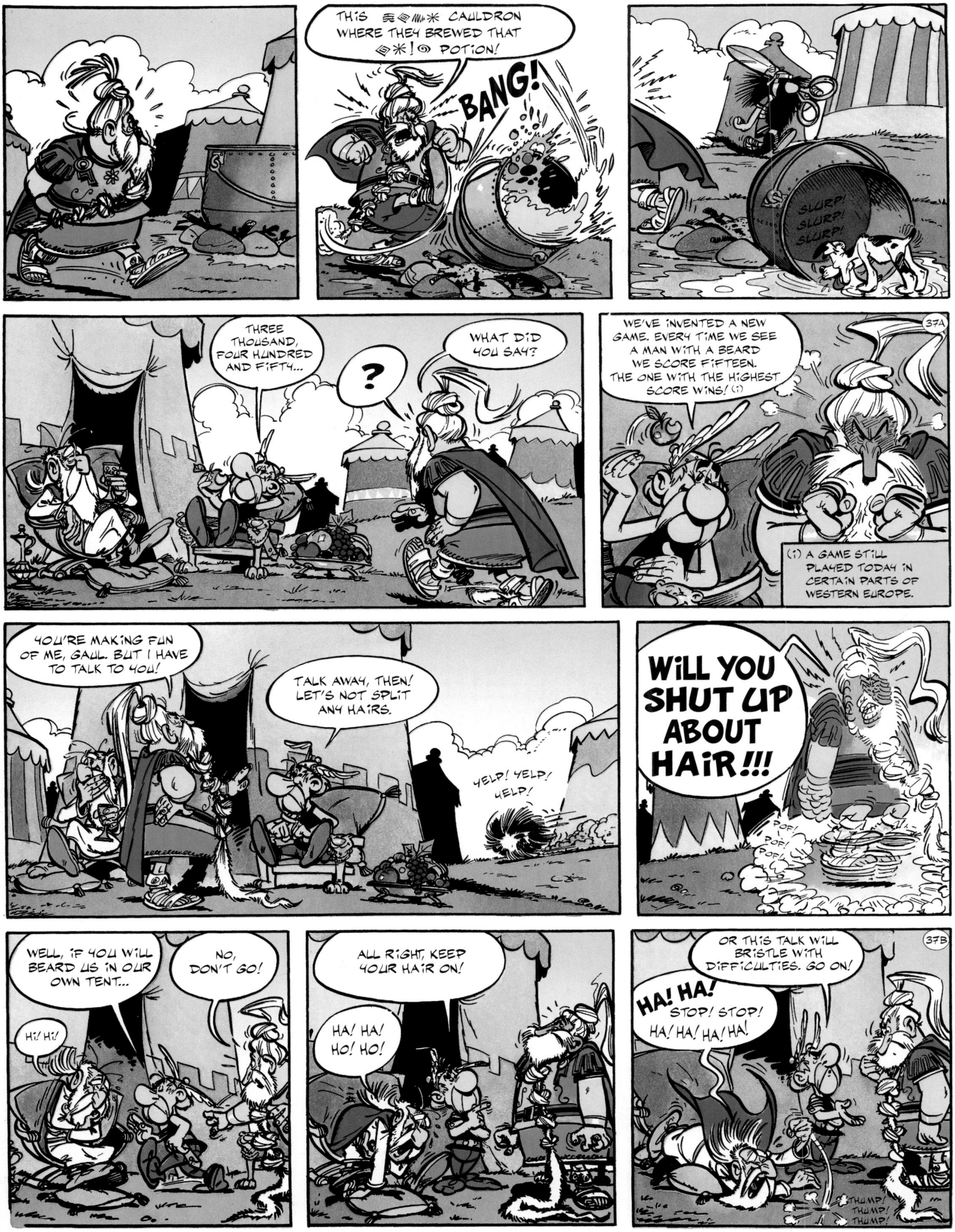

THIS ⚡◎///✳ CAULDRON WHERE THEY BREWED THAT ◎✳!◎ POTION!
BANG!
SLURP! SLURP! SLURP!
THREE THOUSAND, FOUR HUNDRED AND FIFTY...
?
WHAT DID YOU SAY?
WE'VE INVENTED A NEW GAME. EVERY TIME WE SEE A MAN WITH A BEARD WE SCORE FIFTEEN. THE ONE WITH THE HIGHEST SCORE WINS! (1)
37A
(1) A GAME STILL PLAYED TODAY IN CERTAIN PARTS OF WESTERN EUROPE.
YOU'RE MAKING FUN OF ME, GAUL. BUT I HAVE TO TALK TO YOU!
TALK AWAY, THEN! LET'S NOT SPLIT ANY HAIRS.
YELP! YELP! YELP!
WILL YOU SHUT UP ABOUT HAIR!!!
POF! POF! POF!
WELL, IF YOU WILL BEARD US IN OUR OWN TENT...
NO, DON'T GO!
HI! HI!
ALL RIGHT, KEEP YOUR HAIR ON!
HA! HA! HO! HO!
OR THIS TALK WILL BRISTLE WITH DIFFICULTIES. GO ON!
37B
HA! HA! STOP! STOP! HA! HA! HA! HA!
THUMP! THUMP! THUMP!

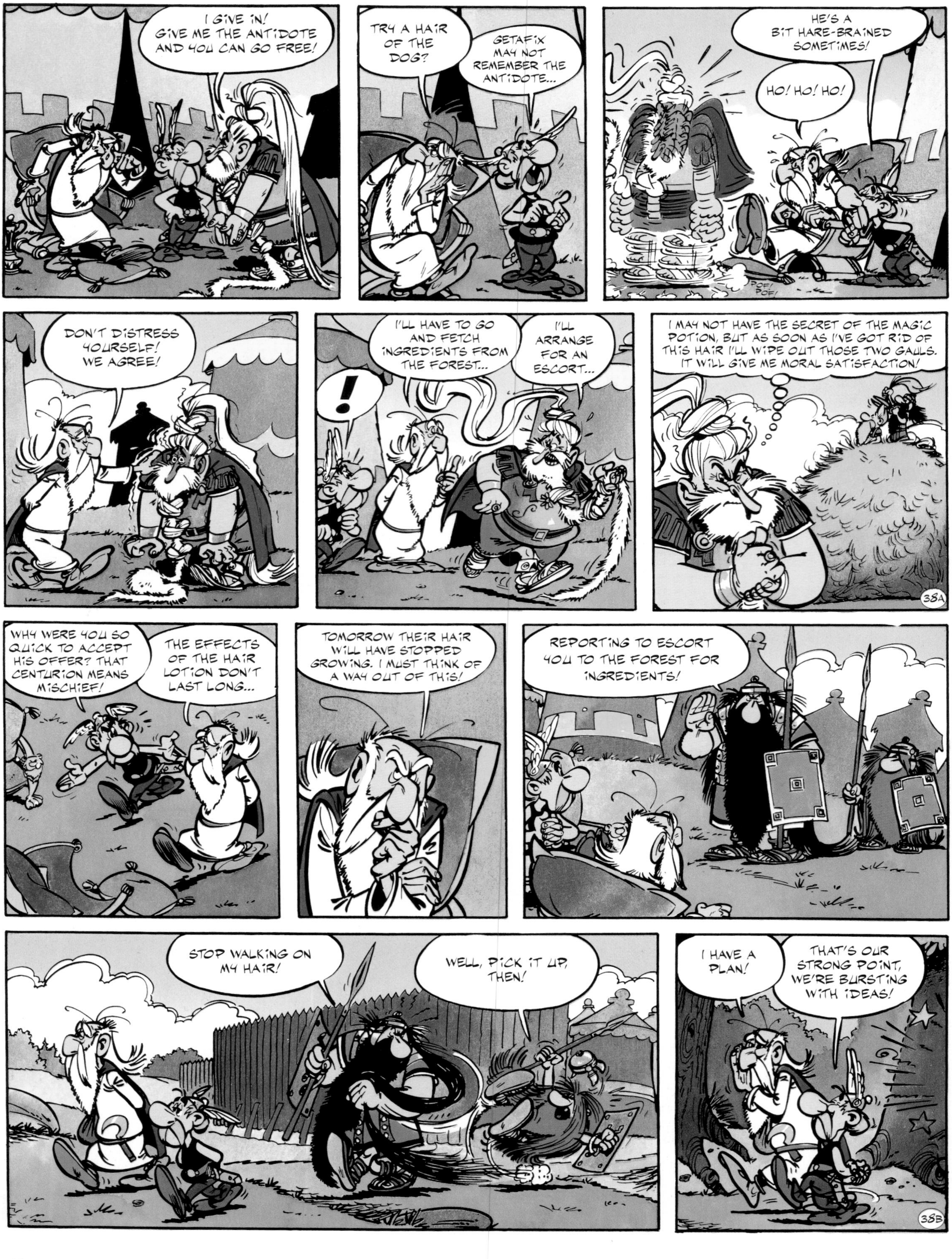
I GIVE IN! GIVE ME THE ANTIDOTE AND YOU CAN GO FREE!
TRY A HAIR OF THE DOG?
GETAFIX MAY NOT REMEMBER THE ANTIDOTE...
HE'S A BIT HARE-BRAINED SOMETIMES!
HO! HO! HO!
POF! POF!
DON'T DISTRESS YOURSELF! WE AGREE!
I'LL HAVE TO GO AND FETCH INGREDIENTS FROM THE FOREST...
I'LL ARRANGE FOR AN ESCORT...
!
I MAY NOT HAVE THE SECRET OF THE MAGIC POTION, BUT AS SOON AS I'VE GOT RID OF THIS HAIR I'LL WIPE OUT THOSE TWO GAULS. IT WILL GIVE ME MORAL SATISFACTION!
38A
WHY WERE YOU SO QUICK TO ACCEPT HIS OFFER? THAT CENTURION MEANS MISCHIEF!
THE EFFECTS OF THE HAIR LOTION DON'T LAST LONG...
TOMORROW THEIR HAIR WILL HAVE STOPPED GROWING. I MUST THINK OF A WAY OUT OF THIS!
REPORTING TO ESCORT YOU TO THE FOREST FOR INGREDIENTS!
STOP WALKING ON MY HAIR!
WELL, PICK IT UP, THEN!
I HAVE A PLAN!
THAT'S OUR STRONG POINT, WE'RE BURSTING WITH IDEAS!
38B

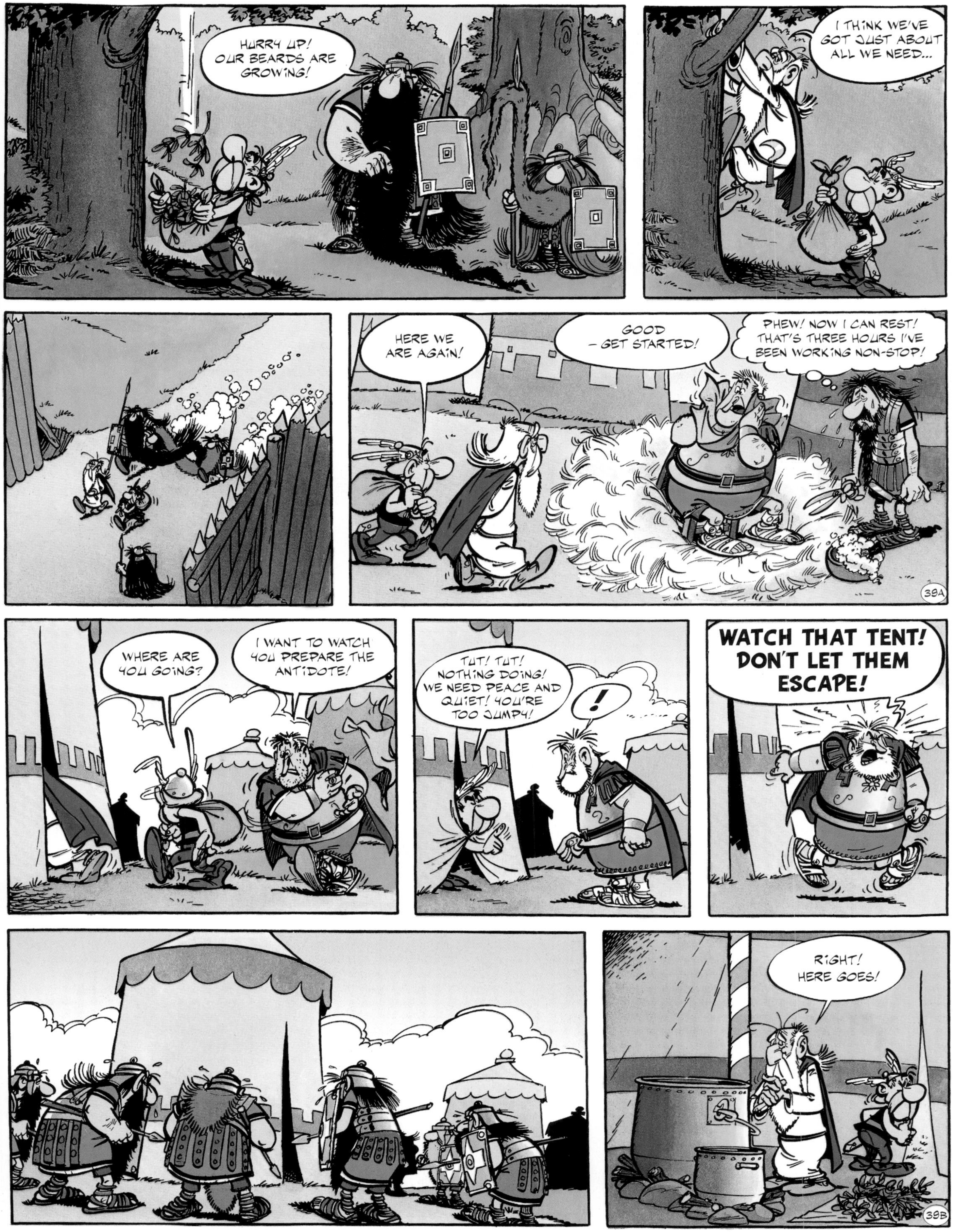
HURRY UP! OUR BEARDS ARE GROWING!
I THINK WE'VE GOT JUST ABOUT ALL WE NEED...
HERE WE ARE AGAIN!
GOOD – GET STARTED!
PHEW! NOW I CAN REST! THAT'S THREE HOURS I'VE BEEN WORKING NON-STOP!
38A
WHERE ARE YOU GOING?
I WANT TO WATCH YOU PREPARE THE ANTIDOTE!
TUT! TUT! NOTHING DOING! WE NEED PEACE AND QUIET! YOU'RE TOO JUMPY!
!
WATCH THAT TENT! DON'T LET THEM ESCAPE!
RIGHT! HERE GOES!
38B

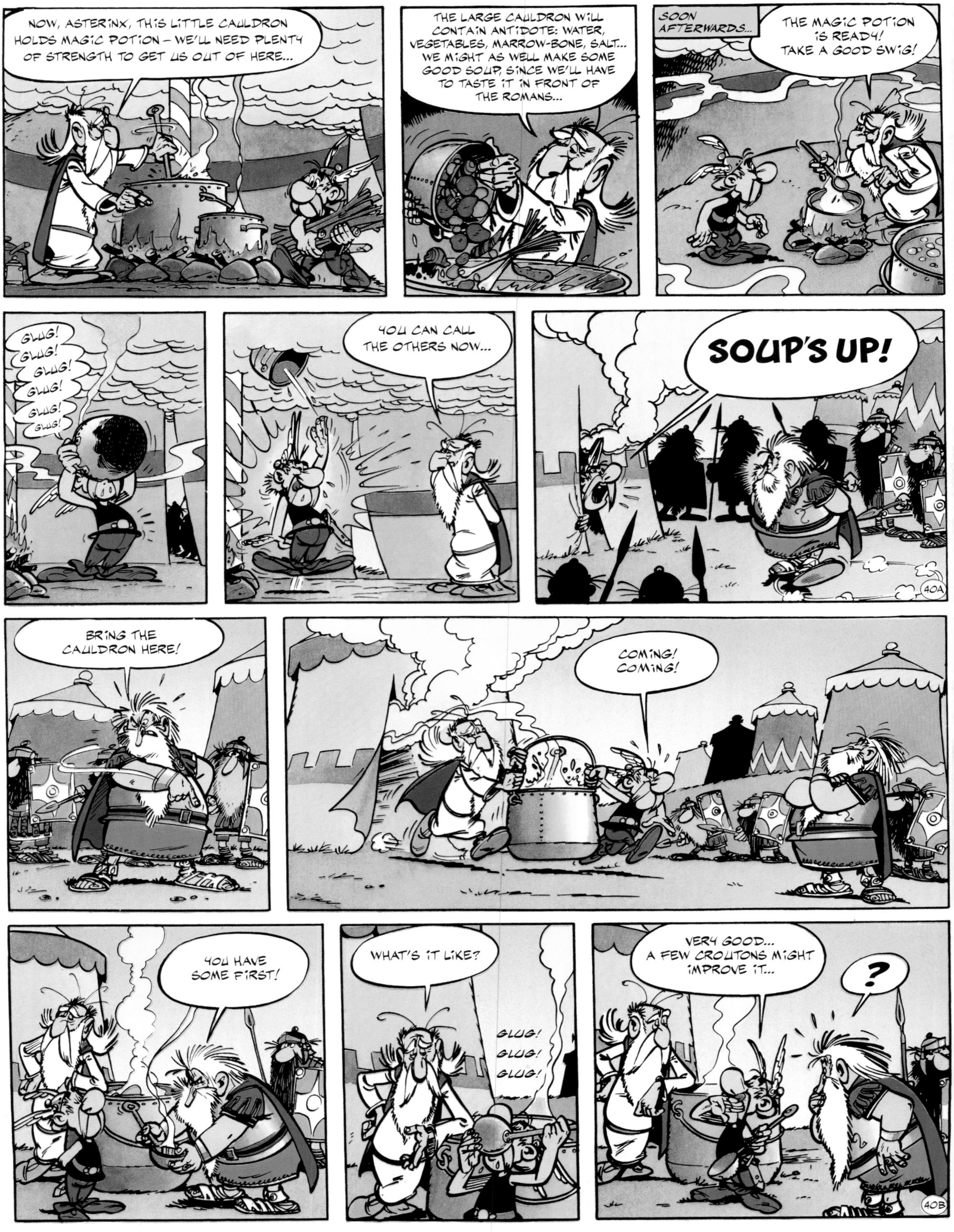
NOW, ASTERINX, THIS LITTLE CAULDRON HOLDS MAGIC POTION – WE'LL NEED PLENTY OF STRENGTH TO GET US OUT OF HERE...
THE LARGE CAULDRON WILL CONTAIN ANTIDOTE: WATER, VEGETABLES, MARROW-BONE, SALT... WE MIGHT AS WELL MAKE SOME GOOD SOUP, SINCE WE'LL HAVE TO TASTE IT IN FRONT OF THE ROMANS...
SOON AFTERWARDS...
THE MAGIC POTION IS READY! TAKE A GOOD SWIG!
GLUG! GLUG! GLUG! GLUG! GLUG! GLUG!
YOU CAN CALL THE OTHERS NOW...
SOUP'S UP!
40A
BRING THE CAULDRON HERE!
COMING! COMING!
YOU HAVE SOME FIRST!
WHAT'S IT LIKE?
GLUG! GLUG! GLUG!
VERY GOOD... A FEW CROUTONS MIGHT IMPROVE IT...
?
40B

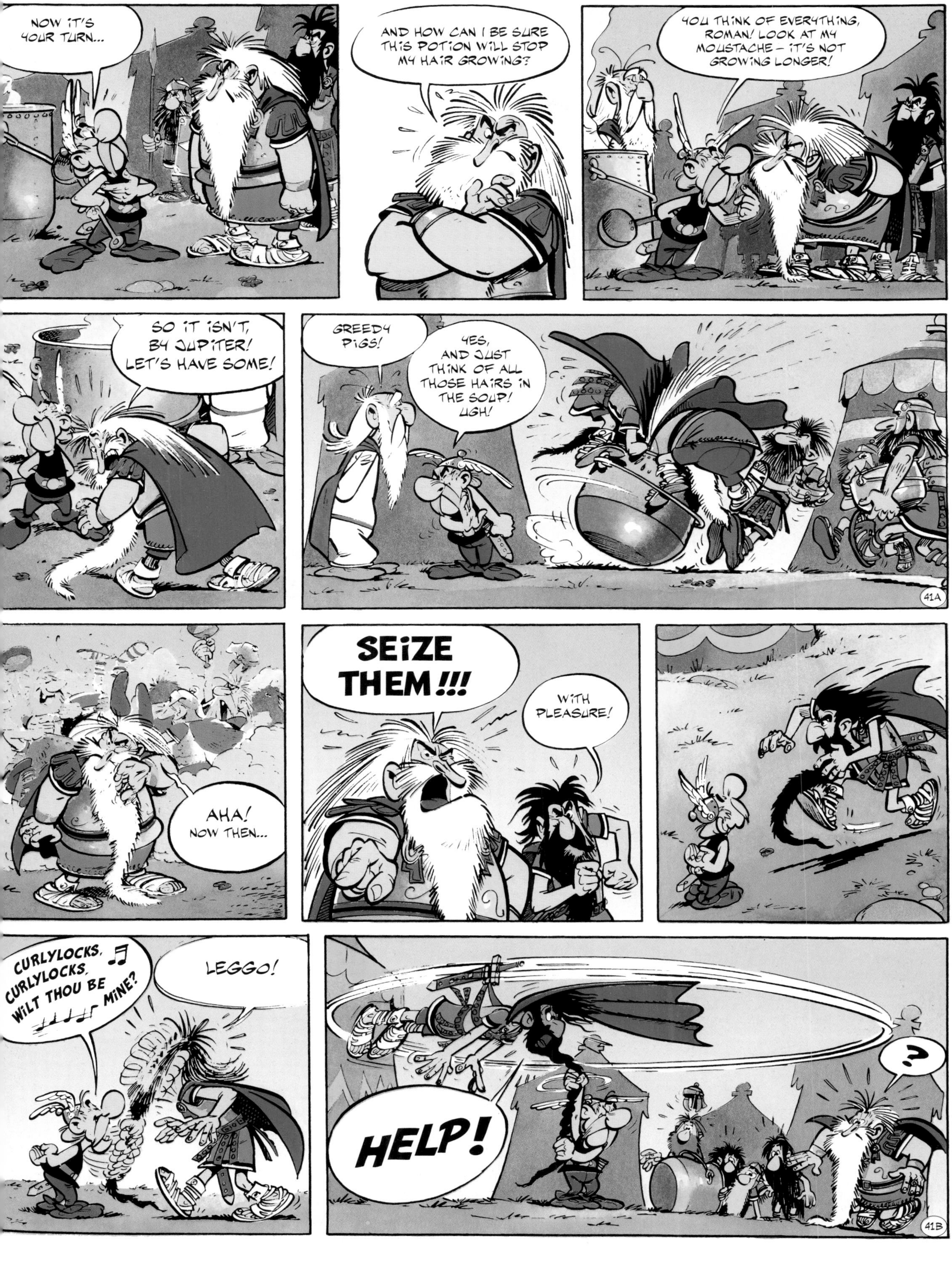

NOW IT'S YOUR TURN...
AND HOW CAN I BE SURE THIS POTION WILL STOP MY HAIR GROWING?
YOU THINK OF EVERYTHING, ROMAN! LOOK AT MY MOUSTACHE – IT'S NOT GROWING LONGER!
SO IT ISN'T, BY JUPITER! LET'S HAVE SOME!
GREEDY PIGS!
YES, AND JUST THINK OF ALL THOSE HAIRS IN THE SOUP! UGH!
41A
AHA! NOW THEN...
SEIZE THEM!!!
WITH PLEASURE!
CURLYLOCKS, CURLYLOCKS, WILT THOU BE MINE?
LEGGO!
HELP!
?
41B

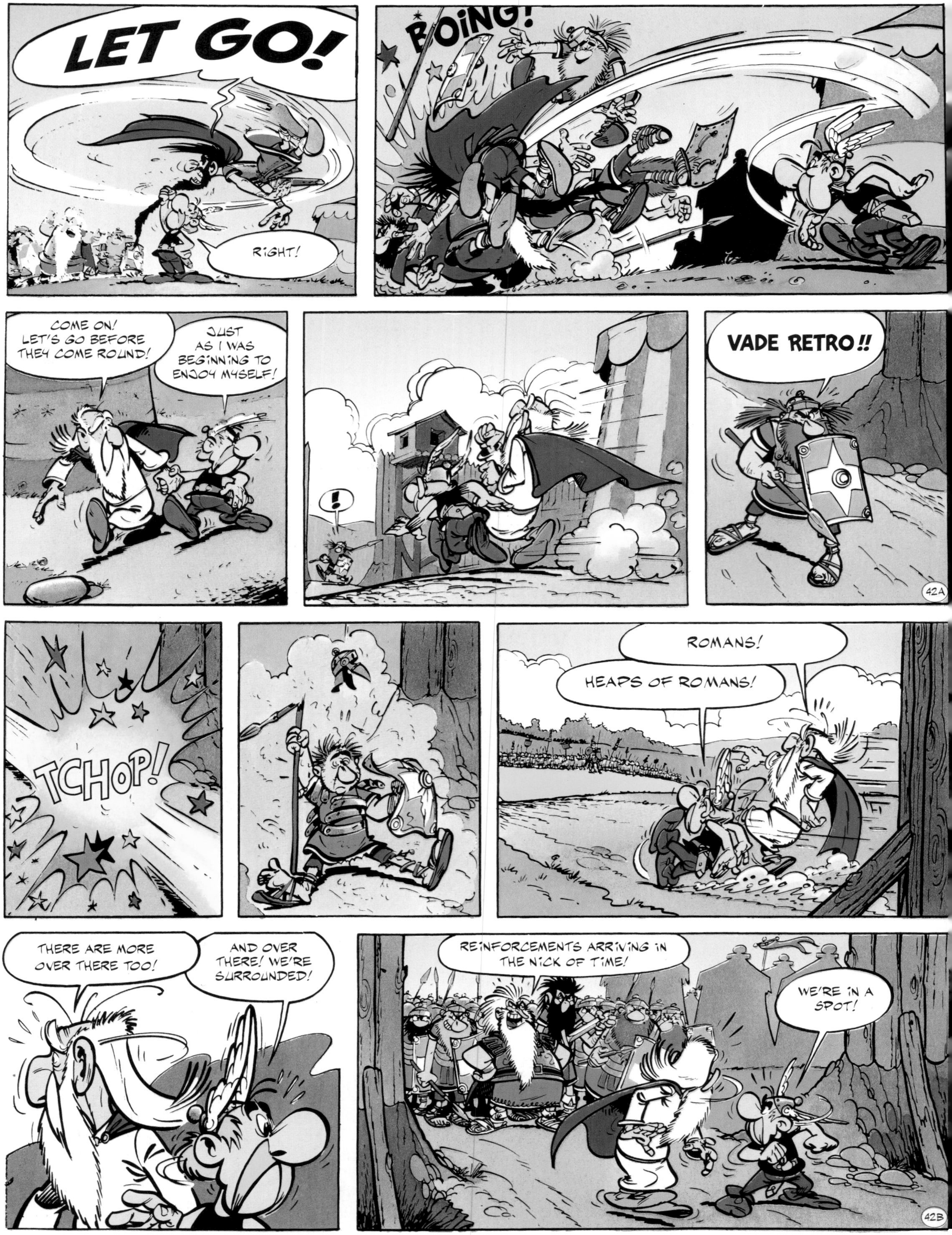

LET GO!
RIGHT!
BOING!
COME ON! LET'S GO BEFORE THEY COME ROUND!
JUST AS I WAS BEGINNING TO ENJOY MYSELF!
!
VADE RETRO!!
42A
TCHOP!
ROMANS!
HEAPS OF ROMANS!
THERE ARE MORE OVER THERE TOO!
AND OVER THERE! WE'RE SURROUNDED!
REINFORCEMENTS ARRIVING IN THE NICK OF TIME!
WE'RE IN A SPOT!
42B

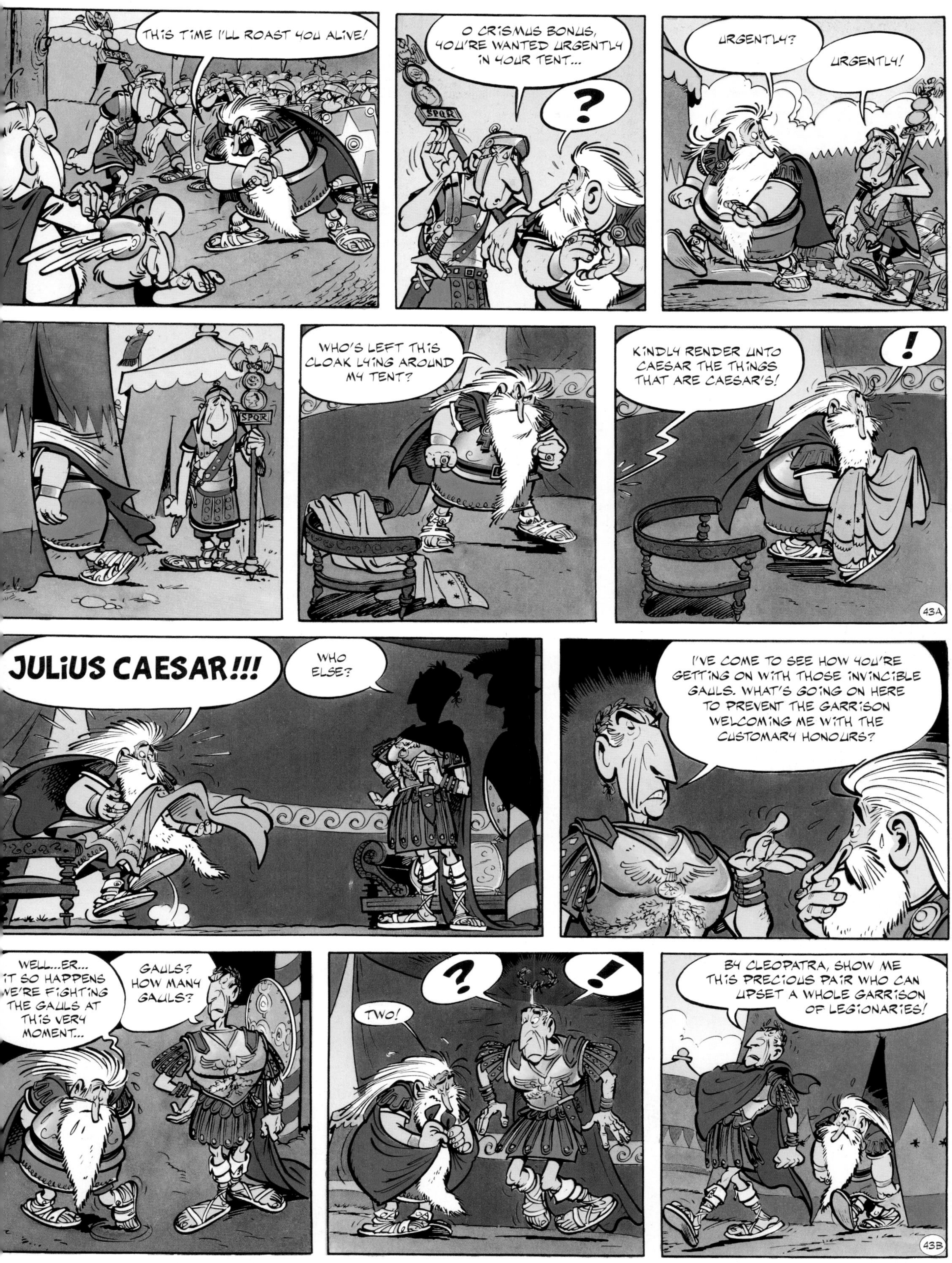
THIS TIME I'LL ROAST YOU ALIVE!
O CRISMUS BONUS, YOU'RE WANTED URGENTLY IN YOUR TENT...
?
URGENTLY?
URGENTLY!
WHO'S LEFT THIS CLOAK LYING AROUND MY TENT?
KINDLY RENDER UNTO CAESAR THE THINGS THAT ARE CAESAR'S!
!
43A
JULIUS CAESAR!!!
WHO ELSE?
I'VE COME TO SEE HOW YOU'RE GETTING ON WITH THOSE INVINCIBLE GAULS. WHAT'S GOING ON HERE TO PREVENT THE GARRISON WELCOMING ME WITH THE CUSTOMARY HONOURS?
WELL...ER... IT SO HAPPENS WE'RE FIGHTING THE GAULS AT THIS VERY MOMENT...
GAULS? HOW MANY GAULS?
?
!
TWO!
BY CLEOPATRA, SHOW ME THIS PRECIOUS PAIR WHO CAN UPSET A WHOLE GARRISON OF LEGIONARIES!
43B

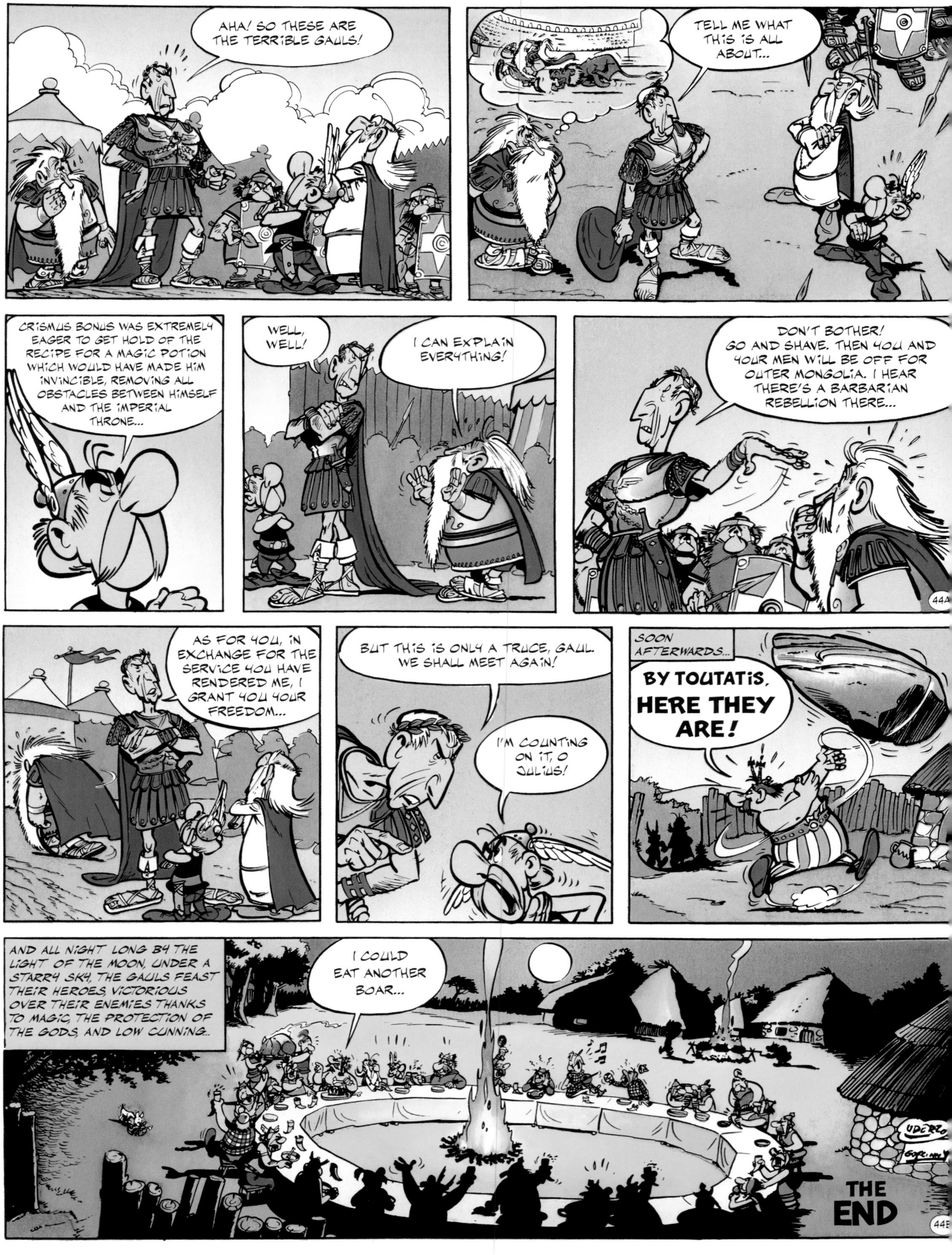
AHA! SO THESE ARE THE TERRIBLE GAULS!
TELL ME WHAT THIS IS ALL ABOUT...
CRISMUS BONUS WAS EXTREMELY EAGER TO GET HOLD OF THE RECIPE FOR A MAGIC POTION WHICH WOULD HAVE MADE HIM INVINCIBLE, REMOVING ALL OBSTACLES BETWEEN HIMSELF AND THE IMPERIAL THRONE...
WELL, WELL!
I CAN EXPLAIN EVERYTHING!
DON'T BOTHER! GO AND SHAVE. THEN YOU AND YOUR MEN WILL BE OFF FOR OUTER MONGOLIA. I HEAR THERE'S A BARBARIAN REBELLION THERE...
44A
AS FOR YOU, IN EXCHANGE FOR THE SERVICE YOU HAVE RENDERED ME, I GRANT YOU YOUR FREEDOM...
BUT THIS IS ONLY A TRUCE, GAUL. WE SHALL MEET AGAIN!
I'M COUNTING ON IT, O JULIUS!
SOON AFTERWARDS...
BY TOUTATIS, HERE THEY ARE!
AND ALL NIGHT LONG BY THE LIGHT OF THE MOON, UNDER A STARRY SKY, THE GAULS FEAST THEIR HEROES, VICTORIOUS OVER THEIR ENEMIES THANKS TO MAGIC, THE PROTECTION OF THE GODS, AND LOW CUNNING..
I COULD EAT ANOTHER BOAR...
UDERZO
GOSCINNY
THE END
44B

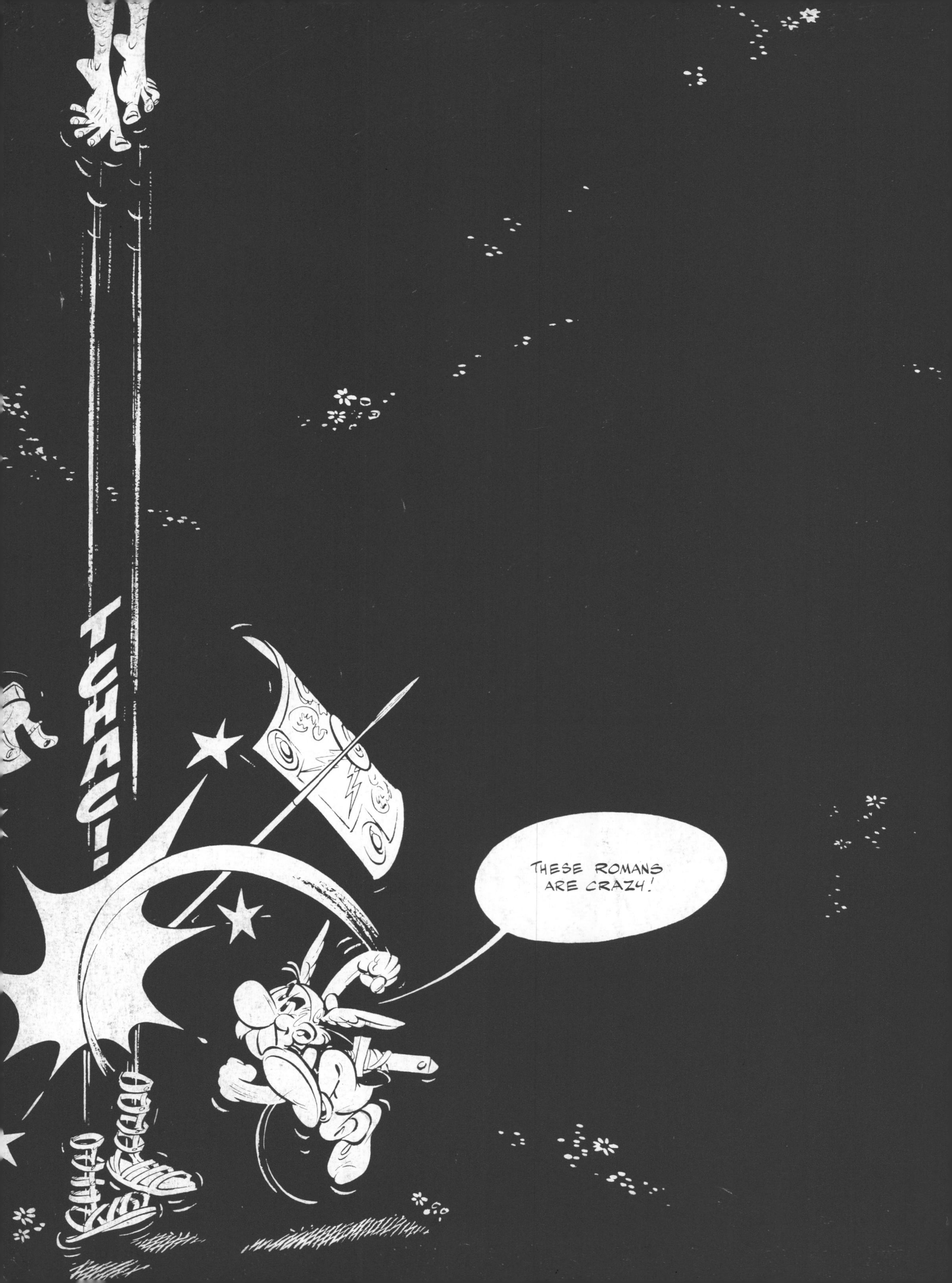
THAC!
THESE ROMANS ARE CRAZY!